Stripper
Lessons

Also by John O'Brien

The Assault on Tony's

Leaving Las Vegas

John O'Brien

Stripper Lessons

Grove Press
New York

Published simultaneously in Canada
Printed in the United States of America
FIRST EDITION

Library of Congress Cataloging-in-Publication Data
O'Brien, John
    Stripper lessons / John O'Brien.—1st ed.
        p.   cm.
    ISBN 0-8021-3507-2
    I. Title.
PS3565.B6695S77 1997
813'.54—dc20   96-44137

Design by Laura Hammond Hough

Grove Press
841 Broadway
New York, NY 10003

10 9 8 7 6 5 4 3 2 1

Stripper
Lessons

Tuesdaywednesday

ark, but not really. In fact when you come in night after night your eyes adjust before the dirty velvet curtain swings almost-closed at your heels, parting into a vertical peephole and making you feel more INside than if six inches of oak had just slammed shut tight at your back. It's when the exit in the rear—EXIT ONLY – NO IN AND OUT PRIVILEGES—is pushed open and the security lights of the parking lot flood the room like sunshine, washing out the red and blue spotlights that some of the girls are partial to, that you realize, or remember, just how dark it really is. True, that door has a big spring on it to make certain that it never stays open by itself, and

the human eye is a remarkable thing, and what he sometimes thinks about is a commercial, TV commercial, say
it was on last night: woman, dripping out of shower, into
bedroom, back to camera, lets fall towel, and you just
gotta buy *some*thing. You just gotta *believe* in something.
And naked is naked. And he wonders, really, if just knowing that they're naked wouldn't be enough. Really. After
all, how hard can you touch something anyway? It seems
like even that wouldn't do the trick, so where's the difference? Think about what will and won't be seen in here.
It's a call made solely by the powers that be, and Carroll
can see well enough to write whether the door is open
or shut.

On the napkin (so far):

> *Think about Nikki.*
> *Think about Carroll.*
> *Think about Nikki and Carroll.*

His pen crawls along the white surface of the cocktail napkin, retracing as necessary those characters that
have the tough luck of falling on a moist spot. The writing is done in lieu of talking, as a way for Carroll to bounce
thoughts out of his brain. It helps assuage the pressure of
the echo. Somehow, the voice in his head, his own silent
voice, isn't quite so clamorous when he's scratching on a
napkin. And when, later, he balls up the evening's napkins and drops them in the tall, scummy garbage can near
the soda-pop bar of this place, he'll feel lighter, as if what
he wrote really was lifted from his mind, or maybe, in a
way, as if one of the dancers took it, accepted it as a secret, romantic missive, and batted her lashes, smiling to

him from across the room as she read it. Not this place, not tonight. Not likely.

Slowing and almost out of space on this napkin, Carroll is not quite sure where to go from here, so he lifts the pen, chews it, taps his teeth, decides to abandon the writing for now. That much, then, is done. Clock ticked, heart beaten, worried plastic pen to pocket. His attention turns more directly to the dancer. She knows how to work her hair, tossing it now for Carroll's benefit with an idiosyncratic coordination of hand and neck, making it, she likes to think, appear slightly longer than it actually is (not that it isn't plenty long on its own). Carroll's tongue, via a half orbit gone long around the inside rim of his glass, manipulates his straw back into his mouth. He sucks on sparkling apple cider, thinking that he might continue writing after he finishes his drink, after the waitress takes away the empty glass. He'll quickly snatch up the napkin before she can read it, but not so quick that she doesn't get enough of a glance to arouse her curiosity. What could she do? Just put another clean napkin in its place, that's what. Just go about her life, never knowing what was written on that napkin that Carroll swept away and kept to himself. This thought makes him grin and feel randy. The dancer has loosened him up. He inhales. From across the sunken stage he overhears the remarks of two other men, apparently strangers but conversing nonetheless.

"Man, I wouldn't mind grabbing myself a handful of that!" says one of the men.

For the answer: "Oh yeah. Yeah."

As much as he hates the sound of their words, Carroll can't help but wish he could join in, speak with these guys, capture, somehow, the secret of their profane prattle.

His ear drifts to another exchange. The man seated nearest him is saying something to the cocktail waitress, who has evidently spilled something on his suit.

"I hope you cook better than you serve drinks," chuckles the man.

For the answer: "He didn't marry me for my cooking." (Laughs)

The dancer works her hair for Carroll. This is her, part of how she sees herself. The gestures are so closely integrated into her every move that if tomorrow she were to rashly cut her hair short it would no doubt take her weeks to break the habit of pulling it off her face. Indeed, he is impressed, and he dutifully adds a second dollar bill to the space that is his on the rail before him, creasing it so that, like the other, it won't fall from its perch. The cocktail waitress glances at his glass, and seeing that it's still almost full, she turns tartly, meanders back to the bar. Carroll chides himself for not drinking more quickly. Nervous, distracted, this was, he promised himself last night, this was to be the night that he tried talking to one of the other customers, one of the other men.

". . . pretty blond hair," Carroll Mine mutters to no one at all, perhaps himself. And then, as if this rehearsal has come off better than expected, he says across an empty chair to the man seated nearest him, "She has pretty blond hair."

The moment hangs like that for just a beat; then with some relief this other man watches his inquisitor abruptly look away, back to the napkin he has evidently written on, guarding it jealously, blocking it with his palm. With some relief this other man sees that a response will not be required of him; the guy has gone back to his writing, has forgotten all about this other man, so he won't have to answer. With some relief this other man returns to himself, looks at his watch and also at the naked dancer before him. "Not all that blond, buddy," he snorts into his glass.

Not quite as loose now, Carroll turns to the dancer and tries to turn on to her. Her face seems to betray some regret over the drawn-out final verse in the song she chose to be her third and final number. Maybe she just dropped the G-string too soon; next time wait for the bridge. She spins low on her heel, simultaneously bending forward in a tricky twist and giving a full view of her backside to the men seated along the rail, which surrounds the stage on three sides. It's a cool move, but Carroll's been coming here long enough to know that she's really making a quick tally of the bills hanging along the top of the rail. He beams as her eye passes the TWO bills in front of him. Her face remains impassive, and he understands that it would be unprofessional for her to openly express the gratitude that she must be feeling upon discovering such a nice little surprise. This is a nice way to talk, he thinks. These girls don't ask for a heck of a lot.

He drains his glass, hushing with a wholly clamped mouth the sudden gurgle of the straw. Ears ever alert for such a sound, the cocktail waitress materializes at his side.

"Ready for another," she asks-says, her inflection point vanished. She's been told that this guy, unlike most of the others, is sometimes good for a dollar on a three-fifty drink. She dips, tray level, her I-only-serve-the-drinks attitude belied by a sheer pink negligee, a whisper of a nipple.

She is not known to Carroll, who knows most of the girls here by sight if not by name. This is not unusual; a place like Indiscretions has what they call a high turnover. Too many times has Carroll arrived for another evening, sure that This Would Be The Night, sure that a certain special girl, usually a waitress (but sometimes a dancer), was on the verge of letting him talk to her, not just thank you, but really talk about . . . about whatever the hell she wanted to talk about, only to find her missing. He might look around, panic growing. *I knew it,* he might think. Finally mustering the nerve that such a situation calls for, he might ask whoever is serving his sparkling apple cider, *What happened to the other girl?* And thus he would receive the inexorable news: *Her? She's gone. I think her boyfriend made her quit.* And only himself to blame.

So the music is too loud here at Indiscretions. So it annoys everybody—the dancers, the waitresses, the customers, the DJ/doorman, the unctuous bosses in white-on-white polyester shirts that are unbuttoned at the collar as well as the belly, everybody—but Carroll. He likes it, and it seems wonderful to him that he should find this little victory here, that serendipity should light on him in this dark place that has become more of a place-he-likes-to-be than anywhere else he's ever been. So it is with a childish glee that he looks up to the waitress, fills his lungs, and responds to better the music, "YES!" making his insides smile and helping him to forget all about trying to talk to the other men.

So the music is loud and long, and the dancer draws on her weeks of experience, draws on her face and pulls it into something of a smile; she will grin and bare it. From the ceiling hangs a short, ring–tipped chain, an unsightly thing of chipped paint and steel that nonetheless looks quite at home amidst the red and blue spots and the sprayed-black ceiling tiles. She grabs it, twirls, swinging on the ball of her left foot with her right knee bent, back arched, breasts large and firm from the forces of the spin, lips parted from the angle of her thighs, buttocks poetic from the fact of her youth. The music is loud. On each of the three walls that stand behind the tables that stand behind the men seated at the three-sided stage is a giant mirror, and her eye skims the surface of each of these mirrors in turn, bouncing here, then the next, another, and back, following her turn, her twirl on the chain, keeping track of her motion the way her ears keep track of the music, making sure she looks good, keeping something for herself, the most personal stare, which is too quick for the men to trace and so keeps them wondering what she is looking at, what she sees. All is well. The dollars accumulate on the rail as the music at last succumbs to its inevitable fade-out. The dancer slows her spin, finally letting go of the ring and standing on her own two feet. She looks great. Carroll watches a drop of sweat roll along her buttock. She looks just great.

"Nikki, gentlemen, put your hands together for the lovely Nikki." This voice, a deep monotone filling the tight air of Indiscretions and replacing the faded music, is followed by a predictable yet always startling thunderous *whack-whack* of the microphone striking something or other as the DJ/doorman rotates his stool from the admission booth to the turntable. "Once more for a lovelylady named Nikki, gentlemen. As with all our lovelyladies, Nikki is available for a topless table dance. Just ask her for details, or any one of our other lovelyladies, for that matter, and as you know, Indiscretions has the loveliest ladies in all of Southern California."

Carroll, still waiting for his drink, has to admit that this is true. As often as he has heard this claim he has reflected on the consistent beauty of the dancers in this club, and so it is now. The loveliest ladies in Southern California, he thinks, lovelier than the Valley, lovelier than Hollywood, probably lovelier than the whole country! He watches the cocktail waitress collect his sparkling apple cider from the bar across the room. The words *topless table dance* are floating in his head. He can't believe that some guys have the nerve to go through with that; he doesn't even have the nerve to ask how much one costs.

The DJ/doorman continues: "Okay, gentlemen, up next is a lovelylady that I'm sure you all know. Put your hands together for the lovely . . . Tina."

The record scratches once, then finds its groove. Tina parts the curtain and emerges on the stage just as Carroll's drink arrives.

"Three-fifty," nags the cocktail waitress.

Tina, thinks Carroll, oh Tina.

Think about your apartment building. Alone thankgoodness in one of two available elevators, Carroll rises interminably to the second of three available stories. He entered the empty car with the usual feeling of relief; nevertheless, he can't help but steal nervous glances over his shoulder, finally giving in and turning fully around to look straight at the dim and hollow space in the back of the car. Alone. There are twenty-four mirrored self-adhesive tiles on the top half of the rear wall in this elevator. Each shares the same tacky veined patina known to its manufacturer as Jungle Mist, and each is fractured save one—and that one has a hole cut smack through the middle of it for no apparent reason, as if it were once part of an abortive plan to mount the emergency stop button here instead of on the button panel where it belongs. The car jolts to a halt and pauses to muster its resources for the opening of the door. It is 2:15am, and Carroll is home.

The door is a simple matter of one lock, and through that, he switches on the light, a frosted bowl-like fixture suspended from the ceiling in a manner fully understood only by the building's maintenance man, who futilely tried to explain it to Carroll during his brief visit last Saturday, arranged two days prior. "Everything okay at your place?" Maintenance Man had asked rhetorically upon bumping—literally—into Carroll on their mutual morning way to the Dumpsters in the garage. "Yes . . . fine." But it wasn't good enough; he needed to say something else, to be more conversational. "My ceiling light jiggles sometimes . . . like it's gonna fall," he said diffidently, trying hard to please. The maintenance man, now knowing that he should've known better, blinked and pressed his lips together, unwilling to accept that it was he, after all, who had been the one to ask. Can of worms, his wife always says. "Umm, I guess I can come up and take a look at it— it's probably nothing (hopelessly waiting for Carroll to agree and call the whole thing off), but if you *really* think there's a problem then I can take a look . . . ah . . . (in desperation) Saturday." Carroll, too intimidated by the greasy beer-bellied man to say no, had simply nodded several times quickly and muttered his way back through the security door. When Saturday finally arrived he was a nervous wreck, fretting over his ignorance of the proper social conduct for a visit by the maintenance man, and settling on a bowl of peanuts to be placed in view for easy consumption but not offered verbally so as to avoid presumption. Nonetheless, with the visit almost completed he heard the word *peanuts* slip out of his mouth in response to the maintenance man's patient dissertation on the esoterica of fixture suspension. "So that's why it looks like it's about to fall—but it isn't. Understand?" asked the man of Carroll's wide-eyed, vigorously nodding face. "Peanuts?" responded Carroll to the man, who was by then folding his stepladder.

So it is with a theretofore unfelt sense of trepidation that Carroll witnesses the lighting of the living room, unable to bring himself to look at the fixture for fear of witnessing the jiggle in a far more advanced stage than that which had been looked at by the maintenance man. He hadn't really thought of it until then, just a chance meeting, a slip of the tongue in an effort to make conversation. Now he's stuck with this light no matter how precariously it hangs. He cried wolf, and that guy will never want to look at his ceiling fixture again. Face it: he'd be a fool to waste his time.

As well the mixed feelings, a given whenever returning home from Indiscretions, prey heavily upon him, overwhelming, in fact, the relatively minor distractions of the light, the maintenance man, whatever. He feels an inner loss, a separation anxiety whenever he leaves the club, and it is only exacerbated by his empty apartment. This though is tempered with a queer sort of anticipatory thrill deep in his gut, the Christmas Eve thrill of his childhood. Already his mind is at work, confidence building and plans being laid. He need only complete another day of work and he will be right back in the music. Sparkling apple cider, girls, things to be said, and perhaps even the will

to say them. Yes, tomorrow could be the night that everything comes together. Tomorrow could be the night that
he opens his door, not alone, but with a girl on his arm.
He'll say something witty (maybe an amusing little apology about the smallness of his apartment), step inside,
turn on the light . . . damn! And pray, that's what! Just
pray that the light fixture doesn't jiggle and ruin the whole
night. Maybe he should pay someone from the outside to
take a look at it. Maybe he should cool it at the club, not
bring home a girl till this whole Light thing blows over.
One stinking little apartment. One crummy little life. A
million things to worry over. Work. His cousin Adam's
wedding Sunday all the way down in San Pedro or some
godforsaken place (just trying to find it will be a nightmare, don't even think about what happens if you do). A
million things.

And this stinking little apartment is fat with solitude,
the absolute opposite of the club; that place lives, and
Carroll bets it would feel crowded there even if he were
the only person in the place. Right now he needs some
noise, so he crosses from his door to the floor-standing fan
he keeps in the corner of the room, switches it on, and
relaxes in the electric hum of its motor, the rush of the air
through its blades, the plenum it provides. He loves this
fan like a brother, though not as much now as back when
he bought it—and it took a lot of work to find it because
they hardly make these anymore. He knows. He spent
three weeks plus searching for one that was this tall, had
this oversized spiral wire cage, one that would be as close
as possible to the one at the rear of the stage in Indiscretions. It had always been there, rarely switched on, innocu-
ous and pretty much just blending in with the scenery, and

he had not paid it any special mind; not, that is, until last summer. It was then that he saw (watched) a dancer named Billie (no longer at the club) mount the fan like a lover. With a start Carroll realized it was on, had been on for some time—how long? He worried after Billie's hair at first but soon found himself enraptured, hypnotized by her body, the sweat on her back, the gyrations of her hips, and whether or not the steel rod of the fan's base felt cold there, in *that* place. Three weeks later he had one. He found it in the Valley at a Handyman's Heaven. "Whaddeya gonna do with this?" the salesboy wanted to know. What indeed. Of course it's just a memento now, all that's left of Billie's stirring performance, and if truth be told, there's less to this story: the original fan, the one at Indiscretions, the one Billie actually danced with, is gone. Vanished. The club was simply without it one night during the winter and it never returned. Carroll didn't have the nerve to ask where it had gone; he just came home that night, sat in the corner, and dolefully stared at his copy, windless and unwarmed by any libidinous pass. Only recently has he begun to switch it on again. Aging, perhaps a modicum of wisdom: he's learned to appreciate this relic of his past.

He hits the sofa and switches on the TV via the little non-clicking rubber nub of an electronic button on the remote. But the unrestrained parade of late-night commercials that assault the bargain air time like a crowd hitting a holiday mall puts him off; it always does. These dubious appeals to some abject lonely troll inside of him, that he should seize the telephone, dial the salacious beauties pictured on their own sofas, getting off on their own phones, really just talking to their own studs while they wait for Carroll to call. They are at the very far end of his spiraled line, imploring, urrrging him to push some buttons, clutch himself, and rape his phone bill. *Two dollars for the first minute,* advises an afterthought of a superimposition on the bottom third of his screen. *Ninety cents for each additional minute or any fraction thereof.* So that would be what . . . three, four bucks? Now a guy in Garden Grove wants to sell him a piano—in fact ANY piano. Evidently there are quite a few to choose from. Hundreds fill the screen, the camera passing over them from above like so many used Toyotas in the recurrent Jax Jalopies commercial that will almost certainly follow.

He taps the remote—*Pfftssszzzz- - - - z*—the screen sizzles, and the phone girls, their studs, and the piano man are laid to waste like so much coagulated bacon grease. Not so bad. Really. Not so bad some nights, but tonight he just can't stop thinking about Nikki and the way she spun around on her heel. That really *was* a cool move! Now that he thinks about it he realizes that the girl has something, that arched back, that poise, that little special something. How did that go now? Let's see: the one foot up like this. . . . No, cause then she wouldn't have been able to lift her. . . . Wait, that's right, she had her thigh tight against. . . . But then how could we see everything if it was like that? He's vexed, and he suddenly realizes that he's contorted on the sofa, half standing in his efforts to recall Nikki's dance. He reddens, jumps up, and goes into the bedroom, where there's a good-sized mirror: he's gotta try this.

Kill the living room light (it's not jiggling it's not jiggling), quickly goes the short trip to the bedroom, and stripped to—let's see—just socks and underwear. Okay. The closet door is positioned twice, then again, until the bare-bulbed sixty-watt, unseen in its interior, creates a spotlight effect: a vertical column of even yellow light emanating. . . . Okay, not at all like a spotlight, but this is what he's got and it's as good as it gets. He checks the space in which he can spin and finds it'll just do if he's careful. No music, that would be TOO much. . . . Okay, music.

Now the clock radio is on, and it sounds just horrible, nothing like the system at Indiscretions. He tries a few experimental prances, sways, and drops his hands to his hips. The floor creaks like it always does, but he's too engrossed in his mimicry to notice. He closes his eyes, returning himself to the club and recalling the picture of Nikki, her performance earlier tonight. It's there, as clear in his mind as his own image is in the mirror before him. He spins low on his heel, simultaneously bending forward in a tricky twist and giving a full view of his white-cotton backside to the latex-painted drywall that surrounds him on three sides. It's a cool move. It *is* a cool move.

Wednesdaythursday

"**M**orning, Carroll."

"Good morning, Mr. Chase."

As the multiple doors of the elevator squeeze to an immutable closure, the double-breasted Mr. Chase leans toward Carroll conspiratorially, indicating with his left pinkie, free from the burden of supporting a Styrofoam coffee cup shared by the other four fingers, that Carroll should do the same. He does, and together they breathe a common air, Armani aftershave laced with coffee from the plume of steam rising out of the cup between them and infused with the reliable scent of the elevator's high-pressure system. Morning air.

"Just Chase. As long as there are no partners around (a clandestine glance around the empty elevator to confirm this) it's just Chase." Then, from behind a Real Nasty grin reserved for those moments of extra-special bonding: "Fuck the *mister!*" Chase snorts; a droplet of coffee peeks out of one nostril.

Carroll titters respectfully. "Good morning, Chase," he says.

But as the elevator bounces to a halt he is admonished by an urgent nudge: *shh!* 11, says the digital display. "Eleven," says Chase–Mr. Chase. This, then, would be their floor.

So the celestial hum of the elevator is replaced imperceptibly with the telegraphlike tickclick of a hundred well-tuned keyboards, as if they were simply different ends of the same noise. In the distance, mostly muffled behind a walnut-veneer door, springs the throaty laughter of a man and his chums; one can almost hear the chunks of croissant strike the open sports pages, soggy projectiles and the business at hand. Walking directly from the elevator to his desk in the file room, Carroll keeps his head low in an effort to minimize the number of morning greetings he must endure before reaching the all-business sanctuary of his workspace: his folders, his labels, his carefully constructed abbreviations for whatever litigation filing is likely to cross his desk, truncated corporate names destined to sour in the ear when fully and properly pronounced by some overly anxious neophyte, all the meticulosity he harbors there that will make this day fly. Zip he goes around the corners, feeling the centrifugal force in his eyes and gut. He can get behind a file cart in these hallways, pick up speed and corner on two wheels, command respect. Coffee-toting associates have learned to listen for that fearsome shopping-cart rattle. Steel on steel, nerves on ice, eyes on the floor.

"Hi, Carroll."

"Hello, Kathy."

"Morning, Carroll."

"Good morning, Ms. Thompson."

"Whaddeyaknow, Carroll."

"Ahh . . . not much, Mike."

"Oh, Carroll, I'm glad you're here. Listen: get yourself settled and come on back with your coffee or whatever. We still can't locate the SoLo/Bombgate file—heck, I'd be happy just to find the litigation clip! Anyway, HE's going nuts in there, and I told him that you and I would put our heads together and figure this out. Okay?"

He purses his lips. There is the usual moment of panic, captured and swallowed and known only to him this time. He knows who's got the file: the corporate partner who, though no longer working on this hoary Morris Bombgate action, brought in So-Lotions Inc. as a client when he dumped his own loser practice to join the firm and since has always kept tabs on *his* baby, now as large as he is fat. He impatiently denied it two days ago, almost daring Carroll with his eyes to ask again, but then his office is such a fucking nightmare of a mess that he wouldn't know if he had it or not. Carroll wishes he had the guts to sneak in there during lunch and just slip away with it, back to the file room where it belongs.

"Okay, Pam. I'll be back in a minute," he says with no particular plan or reason. He supposes they'll rummage through her secretarial bay for an hour or so until something else comes up for her to do.

"Take your time," she sparkles back.

Carroll proceeds to his desk, hearing at his back Pam's boss's importunate groan: "Pammy!"

At five-thirty, with the day's crises either resolved or postponed, he busies himself at his desk, face buried in a correspondence clip as the bulk of the office drains down the elevator shaft and out into the courtyard (L) or more likely the garage (P1, P2). Five-thirty-five and Carroll splits. His red Chevy Vega, oxidized and anachronous amidst its spiffy Japanese brethren, and sitting cozily in the southwest corner of P2, shoots a Quaker State spunk onto the wall behind it before blasting him out of that nasty tomb. West LA straight down to Inglewood, never any point to going home first. Tonight there's just a prudent stop at one of his bank's ATM machines for a couple of twenties, the stuff that change is made of. He carefully folds the little card of a receipt into his wallet for later accounting.

Show Time. The parking lot at Indiscretions kicks gravel on his car—not actual gravel, but rather the funky too-light chunks of aerated detritus that one finds scattered around construction sites or on the shoulders of an interstate. The place is crowded for a Wednesday, and he has to drive almost to the rear of the lot before finding a small space to tuck the Vega into. Key to off, the car shudders once as if declaring the gridlock-plagued journey from his office to be the last straw. He locks his doors and walks up to the club's entrance under the tan Los Angeles sky.

Indiscretions always looks closed in daylight, probably because the heavy front door sits flush and locked-looking against the building, and the flashing lights that one would normally expect outside of such a place are reserved for the dark and so are the favored customers. As usual, during the moment before he remembers that it really is open and that everything's all right, Carroll's heart skips a beat, and just that quickly the sweat creeps to his upper lip, the back of his neck. None of this is helped by the fact that even after almost two years of coming here he still grows instinctively trepid when entering. To him this is still one of the darker places, the rough side of the city, a place where anything can happen, where a man's got to keep his eyes open, his reflexes tight. He passes into the small space between the door and the velvet curtain inside. He stands. His eight bucks is at the ready, and he looks expectantly to the DJ/doorman behind the glass.

"Back for more, eh?" says the DJ/doorman. He says it just a beat too late, as though he's been planning on saying this for quite a while and finally decided that now was the right time.

Carroll is stunned. This is the first time that the DJ/doorman—this one or any of his predecessors—has spoken to him. They always ignore him, and it isn't lost on Carroll when they laugh it up with the other guys who come in, guys whose names always seem to be on the mysterious lists attached to the DJ/doorman's clipboard. "How are you?" he even tried once to a new DJ/doorman, who, thought Carroll, might have been more receptive to such pleasantries. But he was ignored. The guy just talked right through him to the man waiting next in line. "How ya doin', ace," he said.

His eight dollars is no longer in his hand. The turnstile is buzzing come on. Carroll realizes that the DJ/doorman doesn't want him to respond, doesn't care whether or why Carroll is *back for more,* didn't mean the *eh,* doesn't want to talk to Carroll at all—not now, not ever. It was a rhetorical question, and Carroll spots that. He passes through the turnstile, as well the velvet curtain.

Sabrina is on the stage. She's been at the club for about two months, the average stay for a dancer, or so Carroll has observed. He can tell by her nakedness and by the copious bills set spaced along the rail like so many lunch tickets hung before a fry cook that she is dancing her third number in a set of three. The stage is packed— well, there is one seat free, but it looks to be more trouble than it's worth. He knows that he'll outlast the crowd, so he takes one of the seats set in the rear. These really aren't that bad, now and then anyway. From back here he can watch not only the stage, but also the booths reserved for table dances. Heady stuff, those, and he intends to keep his distance. Some guys seem to spend the night there; what that must be like he can't imagine, can't imagine the . . . well, balls. Why even think about it, they must be a fortune. Sabrina's wrapping up. There's Jasmine, Candy. In front there's some girl walking away whom he doesn't recognize (oh good! somebody new, a little treat). He can see Tina's swaying cheeks in a booth (they always leave their panties on for that), no doubt some old goon bury- ing his face in her chest. How much *are* those things?

"The lovely Sabrina, gentlemen, put your hands to- gether for Sabrina. The lovely Sabrina. Coming up, gentle- men, a lovelylady by the name of Melissa. Melissa, coming up with the first of three." There is a pause, the sound of obscured conversation. A brief electronic squeal ends in a pop, and the DJ/doorman continues. "Once more for Sabrina, gentlemen, put your hands together for the lovely

Sabrina. Remember, as with all our lovelyladies here at Indiscretions, Sabrina is available for table dances. You need only ask her, or any girl of your choice, for details. Now we're ready for the first of three with the lovely Melissa. Put your hands together for the lovely Melissa, gentlemen."

As Melissa takes the stage Carroll is keeping an eye open for the new girl. Standard operating procedure, this, for he likes to be on top of the comings and goings at the club; it's one of the responsibilities that go with his diligent nightly attendance. But so far she's nowhere in sight, and this, he knows, probably means that she's in the dressing area behind the stage, either having danced just before he came in or preparing to go on after Melissa. Since he saw her walking away a second ago, it must be the latter; besides, Sabrina had been up there for almost a full set by the time he came in. Yes. That's almost certainly it. The new girl must be dancing next, right after Melissa, who (though he would never tell her this) tends to take forever with her sets. No big deal. He's got all night.

Melissa. Her breasts. What must it be like for her, relating to the world through her breasts, always through her breasts. That's the deal. You look at Melissa and you see her breasts, naked or not, first you see her breasts. Carroll's watched her a lot. She takes off her top as easily and off–handedly as she might take off a jacket. And topless she's totally at ease and confident, like a belligerent guy in a bar with all his friends around. The bottoms are a little different, a little harder, harder in fact than most girls. But come off they do, though never like the top. You can see that she's naked a lot, not just in the club, and she was naked a lot before she ever heard of Indiscretions.

That's it for her. Her breasts are her passport to the world. She needs a date? Here are her breasts. She needs an apartment? Here are her breasts. She needs out of a speeding ticket? Take a look at her breasts. And not just men. Other women as well. Small-breasted women must climb mountains of psychological torment, for what? Have you seen her breasts? Even large-breasted women, beautiful large-breasted women, familiar as she to the syndrome, must first cross that hurdle in the form of a silent communication: we know each other. Men who don't know her: leering at her breasts. Men who do know her: obsessed with her breasts. Women who don't know her: mindful of her breasts. Women who do know her: familiar with her breasts. You want to talk to Melissa? Talk to her breasts. That medium is the message, only bigger.

Melissa must really like her routine, for it varies little. Carroll imagines that this must be the cause of some friction between her and the powers that be, but then her breasts, of course, would go a long way toward winning an argument, even that argument in this place. Melissa, a one-trick pony, does very well here. And for some reason she seems to resent this, seems to narrow her eyes in antipathy at each new bill placed on the rail, looking then to the man behind it as if to catalog the perpetrator. She's been at the club for over a year—longer than any other dancer Carroll can remember. All that time, always the same. Her first song is generally danced in a white T-shirt and panties, occasionally an adolescent teddy: little girl stuff. She'll then disappear behind the curtain (standard procedure) and return almost immediately (most girls wait well into the song), sometimes even before the DJ/doorman can get things spinning. This second number is invariably done with a large translucent off-white scarf. She whips it around and about her otherwise naked body artfully, never exposing simultaneously her top and bottom, front and back. This is pretty tame stuff for the crowd, who by this point are used to being treated to more graphic fare. Then comes the third and final, and she can be expected on stage, again too early, wearing only her disdain. This dance can be downright vulgar, guaranteed to make the men at the stage repent their earlier calls for More Pussy! In fact, it was during one of Melissa's third numbers that Carroll witnessed the only instance of a dancer touching herself—that is, putting a finger *inside*—at Indiscretions. He remembers that the room got really quiet. He felt one with the crowd, mysteriously contrite, and he wished that Melissa would look at him and laugh, or spit, or something.

So why does she stay up there so long? Other girls' sets go by much quicker (they really do, he's timed it). Melissa picks longer songs. She's out there early, lingers too long after her set, just languidly orbiting the inner stage, darting to the rail now and again to snatch up a bill and shoot a sneer at its giver. Actually she's toned it down some in recent months. Maybe the whole thing was just in his imagination to begin with, but these days she does seem sort of beaten. Here she comes for her second song, same old off-white scarf (it couldn't be the very same one?). A guy in a three-piece suit and no tie puts a twenty on the rail, but she just turns away, eyelids drooping. ThreePieceNoTie looks around and laughs: he wants us all to know that this is exactly the reaction that he wanted; he got what he paid for and then some; he's nobody's fool. That guy thinks she loves him, thinks he loves himself.

Melissa doesn't even know he exists. Carroll misses her venom, wishes she would hate us the way she used to.

His eyes dart around the club in their usual circumspect fashion; he hates to be seen seeing. There is still no sign of the new girl.

"—lo," he catches from behind him.

Startled. Spinning . . . no, other shoulder. This must be the tail end of *hello,* and indeed that would follow. It's the new waitress that he first saw last night. He's not sure he likes this girl. "Hi . . . lo," he manages.

The napkin is dropped. His eyes foolishly follow it.

"Sparkling apple cider, right?" she asks, though she is already writing it and poised to walk away.

Okay, that tears it. First the DJ/doorman talks to him, and now a cocktail waitress—a new cocktail waitress—guesses his drink order. NEVER, absolutely NEVER has anything like this happened before. And in the same night! This is some sort of banner day, but is it good or bad? Should he get up and walk out, or would that only make it worse next time he came in. No, if he leaves now he can never come back. That much is clear; maybe it wouldn't be to a less observant person, but to Carroll it is. He prepares an answer. But as before it is too late. The waitress (what the heck is her name?) is gone, gone off to fetch his drink order. His hand is trembling. The most worldly part of him tells him that it's all nothing, that it was only a matter of time before someone here got a little familiar. After all, these people chat and kid with the other men every night, and most of these other guys aren't here half as often as Carroll is. But GOD! how he hates the thought of being included in the group. Loves it and hates it.

Melissa's naked now. Third and final. He tries to concentrate on the new girl. He can smell her beauty. She, at least, won't know him from Adam, won't try to get so damn chummy. Of this he can be certain, and his hand settles down a bit with that knowledge. Melissa is swinging her empty arm around the stage, as if she were still holding her scarf from the previous number. For a moment she looks confused, befuddled, but when Three-PieceNoTie puts up a bill next to his twenty she goes to him, obeisantly squatting with knees wide. He licks his lips, and Melissa's one-word response cannot be heard over the music. Carroll wants his sparkling apple cider delivered before this song is through, so he won't have to deal with the waitress while the new girl is dancing. He looks impatiently at the bar. He can see it sitting on the waitress's tray, she gabbing with the barmaid. The guys are getting competitive around the stage, and this should be a lucrative set for Melissa. Carroll watches her as the music fades out. She stands there for a moment in her nudity, arms loosely at her sides as if waiting for some invisible doctor to tell her what to do now that she's undressed at his bidding.

"Melissa, gentlemen, put your hands together for the lovely Melissa. Remember, gentlemen, that each of our lovely—"

The applause is louder than usual. His drink arrives. Too many distractions, Carroll wants everybody to shut up so he can get the name of the new girl. He pays for his drink hurriedly, waving off the change from a five. This pisses off the waitress, who would rather have coerced this tip out of him with a squint she's been told is very intimidating. Melissa has collected her tips and left the stage.

The curtain to the dressing area billows out. It is holding something exciting, Carroll can tell.

"—together for our newest lovelylady, a lovelylady by the name of Stevie." A heavy exhale resonates through the microphone; then, remembered, it is shut off. The needle skips only once on the record.

No one else looks to be very interested, and Carroll wonders if this could mean Stevie has already danced tonight, danced for them when he wasn't around. The curtain maintains its high pressure, then is parted by a hand, an arm, a leg. Like that the girl is on the stage. The room falls briefly to attention—a blond head will do this. But then some of the men drift back to their conversations, content with glancing at the stage every few seconds as a way to introduce punctuation into whatever it is they're saying. Not them, Carroll is smitten.

Now here's a girl. She is perhaps five feet, seven inches tall with straight blond hair that caresses her shoulders gently. Her posture is implacably correct, as good as the final drawing in any man-from-apes sequence, in the most expensive textbooks, the finest schools. Stevie's breasts push the outside limits of perfect. They loom high and resolute over her narrow waist. She has emerged for this first number effectively naked, wearing only a very short and sheer black camisole with a matching G-string, which reveals her pubic area to be startlingly hairless. To Carroll the vision is stunning, and he loves the fact that she could so iconoclastically snub club tradition on her first dance and dispense with the tiresome routine of Almost-Dressed to Not-Dressed, that she could be so proud, have such confidence in her body. He sees these things, and he adores that she can so quickly lead him to such percipience. But while a striking sight, her to-the-point nudity may be about two songs too early for many of the men, who look disappointed about something they haven't yet identified and uncertain about why they should be. She makes center stage. The music is there and the dance begins.

FirstOfThree—she's lovely. Maybe in pictures, maybe there you can find girls like this. But I don't think so, not in any pictures I've ever seen. This is beauty. Unique. Ineffable. What's the point of description, the point, even, of thought? To sit here, living your life, when suddenly the world changes—how can we go on when we're subject to such manipulation? How can we not? This image of this woman, so ethereal, so very far from any place my hands will ever be, nevertheless is palpable; I can feel her in my GUTS. It's like I could be done here, like I've seen enough. I could just shut my eyes now and never open them again, knowing as I blindly grope through the rest of my abject life that I did precisely the right thing. Like knowing just how much salt is in a pinch, I would be an artist. Or maybe a sinner. Yes, I would be a sinner for failing to deliver my life to the furthest possible pursuit of this vision. I would be a sinner for not seeing her the moment after I closed my eyes. I don't want to be a sinner. I want to do what is right, and everything I know in the world right now, every part of my body and soul tells me that What Is Right is to continue looking at her. My mouth is dry. I am thirsty, but I can't look down to pick up my drink for fear that I will miss it, miss whatever she is at that moment. It would be a betrayal to look away. I will not be thirsty. I will not look away. I will not.

SecondOfThree—she breathes intrepidity. Out of the curtain and back in my face, her gossamer top left behind and probably still floating earthward in the air currents of the room, her bottom still in place, awaiting what may come. Her breasts are unequivocal. He who would taunt her betrays a blasphemous voice. There she walks in hostile quarters indeed, among only enemies and those who seek to defile her—save me. But she fears not even fear itself, and she doesn't run. She knows it is this way everywhere. At once her dance is neither reluctant nor rushed. She neither meets their eyes nor looks away. Regret has never touched her, pain bows down: a trick. I can see how it was for her as she witnessed their leering, jeering cries. I can see her response; it is there for everyone to see through the light fabric hanging from her waist. Where others would have retreated, she advanced, and laid herself bare, put down her razor and so the dare that would— and did!—catch *them* with their pants down, around their ankles like so many masturbating boys caught wiping their fingers. I can see her response. She would not look away. She would not.

ThirdOfThree—she's not me, but what I could never dare to be. With no cloth at all she emerges from the curtain, gaining the stage as if she's done it not twice, but a stellar-trillion times before. I now see that the place where she walks is for her and her only. Prepared by others before her, it will be patrolled by those that follow; they will keep it for her return. There she stands, more naked than I have ever been, yet absolutely untouchable. Her sweat is her garment; mine simply smells. She glistens; I drip. Her perspiration is sweet water, and I would lick it chastely from her feet, would gratefully die for the privi-

lege; she would never allow it. Her beauty is sublime; I
have none. She walks among men; I crawl. And if I were
to recklessly approach her, speak to her, utter a simple
platitude, if I were to give her the time of day, ask for it, if
I were to gently cough while crossing her path, breathe
while standing near her, and if she were to answer, respond, look up, acknowledge me in any way, she would
not hate herself for it; I would. Though some things are
beyond my control, and our eyes may someday meet—
dare I say—in the brief and mutual recognition of one
human to another, it would be a tragic mistake. We could
not be the same. We could not.

"—lovelylady by the name of . . . of Stevie, gentlemen, put your hands together for our newest lovelylady
here at Indiscretions . . . Stevie!" The patter of the DJ/
doorman resumes for most of the room. Elsewhere it's
reduced to a keyword in pricked–up ears: ". . . Stevie . . .
Stevie . . . Stevie. . . . "

Stevie, thinks Carroll. And as Jasmine takes the stage
he thinks, Stevie. And later as Candy, compelled by curiosity about the geek-who-suddenly-forgot-to-sit-at-the-
stage-and-tip-after-all-this-time, pinches a nipple solely
for Carroll's benefit, he still thinks, Stevie. He waits patiently for the show to roll over, set after set. Three bottles
of sparkling apple cider are stacked before him, placed
there by the opportunistic cocktail waitress who picked
right up on his agreeable disposition and is happily lib-
erating fives from him along with each absent, drink-
ordering nod. She is pushing the Envelope as well as the
cider, and the manager fairly twinkles in delight over her
spunk, vowing to himself that he'll have another crack at
her late tonight. Finally Sabrina is up for her set—she was

dancing when he came in tonight—and he knows that the cycle is complete. He need only wait through Sabrina and Melissa, then it will be HER again. The name echoes even more loudly at the realization. SHE will dance again, he thinks, Stevie.

He is not disappointed, watching as she again goes through her set. He is rapturously dazed, wearing a face not unlike that of a long-interned hostage glimpsing his wife on the tarmac, a point of entry. This time Stevie's set is slightly different, varied appropriately in small matters of timing and costume, but not so much that Carroll would notice or care. She can do no wrong in his eyes. Her message is delivered; she may choose to repeat or alter it at will. There's plenty of room for writing on the stone tablet of Carroll's heart, and he is predisposed to adore each move and every choice she makes. He is also terrified, terrified when she looks his way, though these occasions are admittedly few and far between. However, that is small stuff, no real problem for Carroll, who is such a master of the averted glance that he responds reflexively despite his bedazzlement. The one exception, the one justifiable excuse for briefly departing the apparition is that. God forbid their eyes should meet.

The truly close call comes later in the evening; in fact it is the last show of the night. Sabrina is hurriedly finishing her set, bowing absurdly facing the curtain and probably wrapping up her last song a bit too early for the sparsely seated diehards left in the club. She has a trick lined up. Shadow man, he waits even now at the Airport Sheraton, and she needs to do him quick and get home without pissing off her always suspicious boyfriend. This is very unusual, strictly taboo as far as Indiscretions is concerned, and if she were busted the best-case scenario would be walking papers from the club and a rep that she's so far avoided, local blacklisting more likely. As far as she knows she's the only girl currently at the club who tricks, and even she hardly ever does it. The bread from dancing here is just too good. But the kind of money offered her tonight and the guy who was writing the figure on his cocktail napkin were both too sweet to pass up.

So Sabrina's off the stage early, apologizing to an annoyed Melissa, who hates last-minute surprises. Stevie is in the corner of the dressing area, waiting for her final set and full of first-night cooperation.

Counting on this, Sabrina whisks to a squat in front of her and says beseechingly, "Honey, I've got to book a few minutes early. It's no big deal around here, but we do always cover for each other and you ought to get used to how it works. So if anybody's looking for me just tell them I wasn't feeling too good. Okay? Please?"

Stevie nods: *sure,* seeing through it and not really caring. Melissa, ready to dance, goes and stands by the curtain. She doesn't want to know.

Carroll's problem really begins during Melissa's first song. The manager, unable to find Sabrina and wanting to talk to her about a last-minute schedule change, sticks his head in the dressing area.

"Hey! Great first night! You seen Sabrina?" he asks Stevie.

"She wasn't feeling well. She said to tell anyone who asks that she had to leave early." Standard from other gigs, this is about the most risk-free response that Stevie could think of, neutral fare from the new girl.

The manager frowns, vexed. "Okay, tell ya what: I gotta stay up here and change the record cause the boy's dumping the bar trash. How about you running back real quick and checking the ladies' room for me—I hate to go in there anyhow. Maybe we can catch her before she leaves."

She's already gone, you fat fuck, thinks Stevie. "Should I really go out there in my costume? It isn't much," she says, looking down at the same little nothing she wore for her first set.

But the manager, now coughing spontaneously, waves her off. "Yeah, sure. It's fine, the place is empty. Hurry back. I'll hold Melissa an extra minute with the record change. You'll have plenty of time." He turns away, adding over his shoulder, "Great first night! Really!"

Stevie isn't thrilled with the idea of being out on the floor in a costume, especially this one, which she wears only when she wants to get attention. But the place *is* dead, and she knows better than to throw what will be seen as Attitude on her first night. Sabrina's gone anyway, and to play this out she need only stick her head in the bathroom and holler. She'll make it quick.

Bridled by the evening's unforeseen distraction, not to mention wanting to keep a safe distance, Carroll never did move forward to occupy a seat on the stage as they became available; rather he remained all night in his original seat in the rear, specifically in the rear on a path that runs from the stage to the ladies' rest room. So there he sits almost too preoccupied with anticipation of her next set to notice and anyway knowing the club too well to ever expect an on-deck dancer to appear on the floor, when Stevie materializes before him, wearing only her sheer and tiny costume. Actually, she's still a few yards away but closing fast, and Carroll is quite literally paralyzed with fear, panicked to the point that, though the idea of meeting her eyes is as preventable as it is unthinkable, he cannot even divert his gaze from her face. Fortunately her eyes are fastened on the door behind him. She is evidently on a mission of mercy, but it won't be long, he knows, before she is on top of him. Their eyes will meet. She'll wait for him to apologize, but he won't know what to say, and she'll be forced to say . . . well, to say whatever she would say in place of the annoyed *excuse me* he would hear from anyone else.

But succor arrives from an unlikely source, as Melissa, spotting Stevie walking away from the dressing area, and unable to tolerate another anomaly in her evening, calls to her from the stage, "Hey Steeevinnn, the plan is to wait backstage when you're next up!"

Stevie turns to her accuser. Melissa has stopped-dead her dance and stands half naked, left hand clinging naggingly to her bare hip like a just-laundered sock to a sweater. A pair of the few remaining men giggle, and she hisses them quiet from the side of her mouth.

"Ahh–," begins Stevie.

"Way!" adds Melissa, needlessly interrupting.

Overloaded—way overloaded—Carroll emits an odd squeal and bolts for the back door. He fires up the Vega, quits the lot, one yellow light. He's going home.

Thursdayfriday

Wee hours, albeit swelling with yet another new cycle. There's always another day to be swallowed. All the projections of doom, years, lifetimes of hawking Armageddon and evil empires: just a con. Too easy, a get-rich-quick keeping us from the horrible truth: everything gets done one click at a time. In his bed, Carroll has the most vivid and cogent dream of his life.

He is sitting naked in an enormous hot tub. His father is with him in the water, and through the rising steam he sees that his dad—in reality a gray man of sixty-two at Carroll's birth and dead by his seventh birthday—

is young and handsome, no wrinkles, jet-black hair. Carroll recognizes him from pictures taken in younger years, holding infant siblings known only as adults to Carroll. There is an unspoken warmth, like the water, between his dad and him, but again, the memories are not there to support this. Nevertheless, it all feels perfect. Suddenly Carroll becomes aware of a third presence in the hot tub; indeed, he and his father have been sitting as if on points of a triangle. It is a girl. Though she is right in front of him, Carroll cannot make out her face, but he knows she is beautiful. She rises spectrally from the water, exposing her naked breasts, stopping when the water is at her waist, but this seems incidental: Carroll knows she has nothing to hide. There she waits, gently hovering at this unlikely height. "What are you?" asks Carroll. The girl smiles at him, ineffable reassurance. "I'm an angel," she says. "You're an angel?" asks Carroll. "Yes," she says. The water, the steam, Carroll now realizes that tears are streaming down his face. "Then I want to ask you something," he says. "Okay," she simply says, all peace, all accepting. Carroll sees that she is now rising further out of the water. He watches the water fall away from her thighs, her gentle pussy. "Will the meek inherit the earth?" he asks.

But if she answers at all he misses it, or perhaps simply doesn't remember as he awakens to his still-dark apartment. It's 4:38am. He's up. For the first time since he's lived here he hears no noise from the street. Then a boom car thunders through the distant air, and Hollywood resumes around him. Moved by the vision of his dream, he feels alone, feels the need to share his humanity, feels afraid of the dark, and this takes him to the only place he has at this late hour: his television. It's in the other room on a short particle-board bookshelf, a box of stubby utility candles kept on one side because they would be easy to find there in the event of a blackout, and another box of the same kept on the other side because they were two for a buck during K'mon-n-Mart's Bargain Daze.

First there is the always unsatisfying and unconfirmed push of the electronic button on the remote. A burst from the center of the screen, it widens to life: pure aggrandizement. Hello: a black-and-white movie in which he recognizes no one. Non-click: static. Non-click: something with captions in Farsi. Non-click: looks like a *Twilight Zone.* Non-click: static. Non-click: static. Non-click: a phone number, undoubtedly Jesus's. Non-click: nobody here but us car salesmen. Non-click: static. Non-click: static. Non-click: a fitness show with six women. He settles for this until a thick-chested guy shows up looking like their fitness pimp. Non-click: static. Non-click: music videos. This will do.

Lots of promises here. Amidst these songs lie the specious whispers of love in his future, flesh in his face. These guitar-strangling boys with voluminous hair that cries loudest in its length and seems already to be thinning threateningly on top are howling for the girls who will faithfully show up in the little movies that flicker between choruses. The story is told. It could be your story. *These* could be *your* girls! What would that take? Stay tuned (we are harnessing the machine). Please stay tuned (we are grasping this awesome power). But really, these girls don't make much sense in the light of Stevie, and to that end, after a party-line ad whose small-print super-briefly warns of an unprecedented five-dollar-per-minute charge, comes a spot that captures Carroll's attention.

"Women. You can meet them," advises one of them, a woman. She is somewhat attractive and sitting in what is meant to be a restaurant, though it clearly isn't. Then she dissolves into another woman, lying prone on a sofa, who agrees, "You can meet them. You can meet US!" Moving nothing but her mouth, she manages to squeeze her cleavage and adds coyly, "I like shy men best." Finally, as if to lend credibility to the claims of these females, a man, wearing a suit and sitting on the front of a desk, conquers the screen like he's here to stay and confirms, "You *can* meet women! All *kinds* of women! IT JUST TAKES THE RIGHT TOOLS!" With this startling pronouncement he reaches to the desk and, without looking, picks up a small box. It's a videotape, and as he continues, its cover fills the screen. "The Shy Man's Guide to Meeting Women," he reads along with us from the front of the box. "Yes, this is the one you've been hearing about. It's all here: The Approach; Just Talk to Her; How About Your Place?; The European Way; and much, much more. Step by step the Guide takes you along, at your own pace, to that magic place you've always wanted to go but thought was reserved for 'other guys.' No more! Chockfull of interviews with sexy ladies who tell you what TURNS THEM ON, what they LOVE TO HEAR from a man. You'll learn, as I did when I first ordered the tape—that's right, I'm a graduate—that you DON'T have to be handsome, that you DON'T have to be rich. Women want just what you want: to have a good time. Sound incredible? It's all on the tape!" Back to the man, now seated authoritatively behind the desk: no more Mister Nice Guy. "I think you'll agree that thirty-nine ninety-five is a bargain. . . . What? You say that's a lot of money? Well of course it's a lot of money to guys like you and me who work for a living. But ask yourself: What are you really working *for*?" A pause, his face lights up: he's gonna work with us on this one. A smile: Monty Hall. "Okay. You're right. Guys like us don't have yachts to mortgage or movie studios to auction off. Tell ya what: call me up at this number (a telephone number bites off the bottom of the screen) RIGHT NOW, and I'll send out your copy of 'The Shy Man's Guide to Meeting Women,' new in the box, for only twenty-nine ninety-five, AND I'll give you a thirty-day money-back guarantee. That's right. If you don't meet more women over the next thirty days than you have in the LAST YEAR! . . . then I'll send you back your lunch money." This last line is added like a challenge. His arms fold over a veritable paragraph of superimposed details, which no doubt relate to the guarantee; then the phone number returns, chasing them away. The man returns. He is standing behind the phone number with the two women from earlier in the ad, one on each arm. "Order now," he entreats. "That's sound advice . . . from a Winner!"

Carroll impulsively starts repeating the number under his breath while he jumps to the kitchen counter. There he writes it down, not really knowing why but aware that he's been given a vision tonight in his dream, and if this strange commercial is a way for him to understand that vision then he'd better follow up. Bigger than him. Pieces to a puzzle. A mission in this madness. He received an omen once and ignored it. . . . Actually, that's not true. . . . Well, he's not sure. To date he's never believed past what he can see, touch, feel. God never called, so why should Carroll answer? But this seems different. Very different. One doesn't fuck with angels. He picks up the phone.

"Concept Marketing." The voice is a woman's, and he wonders if it's one of the girls on the commercial.

He's really on the phone now. All nerves. Perhaps he should have waited; this girl sounds tired. In an embarrassed whisper, he asks for the tape, having to repeat himself twice. This girl really is tired. He hears keys tapping, like the computers at work. Maybe he should hang up and call later. Maybe the man would answer then.

"I'm sorry, sir, but we're not accepting any more orders for that particular item. Now if you'd like—"

"But I just saw the commercial! He said to call right now!" He stops, shocked that he interrupted her, and hopelessly tries to think fast of a way to take it back.

But she undoes it for him with her tapping. "Sir, I am showing that item as now available in stores. If you'll tell me your zip code I can give you the location of a nearby K'mon-n-Mart store where that item is available."

I wonder if this *is* meant to be, he thinks after replacing the phone in its cradle. K'mon-n-Mart is perfect; he can get a VCR there as well. Today. During his lunch hour.

There's still plenty of time before he needs to prepare for work, so he returns to his sofa, very much awake yet not really listening to the broadcast, which waxes religiose.

Sitting at his desk later that morning, Carroll's mind drifts back to the missing SoLo/Bombgate file. He's not sure why—initiative and diligence are largely discouraged at the firm—but it would be nice to knot this little loose end, at least until it comes undone in a couple of days when the file disappears again. To that end he first makes a perfunctory call to Pam, extension 455, so if the need arises he'll have a witness to later substantiate his good intentions; in any case, he'll bail out at the first sign of a problem. Then he waits for noon, busying himself with the chronology of a dead file on its way to the archives. He'll just have to take a late lunch today.

By twelve-thirty he's upstairs on the twelfth floor, the undeclared domain of the firm's senior partners. At this hour the place is predictably devoid of life, the partners being always willing to demonstrate to a client their ability to cut through a peak-hour waiting list at the local restaurants, their secretaries compelled through watch-glancing hints of impending post-lunch projects to dine concomitantly, preferably in the courtyard. Carroll moves swiftly around the bend, slows while passing the empty . . . ? Yes, it is empty. He stops and turns back, just beyond the unoccupied office wherefrom he expects to emerge with the elusive SoLo/Bombgate file.

Heart pounding (what am I afraid of?) intractably, he enters the office. This guy better be at lunch. He's used to anxiety, even terror on a daily basis; what really catches him off guard is the hitherto unfelt exhilaration of defiance, deep inside, tickling his gut with the tongue tip of *no!* instead of the feather of fear. But emotion notwithstanding, this search won't be at all easy or reflexive. The name So-Lotions Inc. garnishes almost every scrap of paper in this corporate jerk's life, and as much as he doesn't want to risk being seen examining documents, finding the neglected Bombgate litigation will take more than quick glances. Hopefully there's some order to this mess. Hopefully the guy eats like he looks.

Carroll starts with the left side of the credenza, a likely place for things misplaced: Harper Fos— No. So-Lotions Inc. Quarterl— No. So-Lotions Inc. vs. Westcros— No. PolySec— No. So-Lotions Inc. 19— No. So-Lotions Inc. vs. Sunlution— No. General Sta— No. So-Lotions Inc. Cayman Is— No. So-Lotions Inc. Minu— No. So–Loti—

"Everything in order, sport?" booms a challenge from the door, startling Carroll into a gasp of confession. The man's face is tight and red, his tone laced with enmity. Shirtsleeves. Jacket still hanging behind the door. Plain as day. Should've noticed. Dumb.

"Um . . . actually . . . I was looking—"

"Yes, yes, Carl, I know you're from the file room. If you're in need of something I'd appreciate it if, in the future, rather than rummage through my office, you'd simply call my secretary and— Say, you're not still looking for that litigation file, are you? Tell me you're not in here looking for something I already told you I don't have!" This guy is really fat.

Really, Carroll notices. "Um . . . SoLo/Bombgate, it was. Yes—" Dumb.

"Dammit! After I took the trouble to help you locate a file that your department lost? Are you saying that you didn't believe me? Is that it?"

Carroll can't think of anything to say. After all, that *is* it.

Trying unsuccessfully to temper himself: "Look, Carl, I don't have time for this right now, and I should think you wouldn't either." Newly enraged at the notion of employee indolence: "Dammit! Why the hell are you wasting time on this? Why do you care about this file? Don't you have WORK to keep you busy during the day?" Finally, drooling with implication: "Everyone else around here seems to!" And leaving unspoken: *Or maybe you shouldn't be around here?*

And for the briefest instant Carroll has the insane urge to ask him if he has SoLo/Westcross anywhere in his office, just so he can wave it in that fat face after the guy denies it. You Fat Fuck. "Sorry, sir," he mutters instead, on his way out. Says it again for no apparent reason upon leaving the eleventh floor, returning to his desk on ten.

But he doesn't linger at his desk for long. Not only does K'mon-n-Mart, his lunchtime errand, beckon, but he would just as soon avoid a follow-up phone tirade from upstairs. So he's fleeing for an hour . . . sort of. . . . The thing is: it's kinda more about procedure than it is about actual fear. Circumstances dictate that he should split for a while. In fact that scares the hell out of him. He should be absolutely, positively, frightfully shaking. Trembling, vIbRaTiNg with the strings, he should be. In the throes of a breakdown, he should be. But none of these, he is. Maybe it'll hit him later. Maybe this is so much worse than, say, a jiggling light, that it can't even be addressed in the same universe of dread. Maybe later today he'll be sitting at his desk or walking down the hall and he'll just *pop,* just fall to the floor whimpering, spend the rest of his life in a mental hospital. Already his hand is shaking, and. . . . Fuck it. He drops the pencil he was worrying. He's got a videotape to buy.

And at the K'mon-n-Mart Carroll comes to pass a self-standing corrugated cardboard point-of-purchase display dedicated exclusively to the promotion of "The Shy Man's Guide to Meeting Women." And at the base of this display, unseen by Carroll or by any other, is the twisted black ember of a discarded match, smoldering, near dead, and unable to ignite the flame-retardant coating of the cardboard, which only chars two millimeters inward from one acute corner. And on the display the tapes are laid apart on two wings, each given the measure of three tapes across and four tapes down. And Carroll first selects a tape from the left wing but then replaces it in favor of one from the right wing because, after all, it is the right wing. And while he intended to make one single combined purchase of tape and VCR, this cannot be done, for the tape must be paid for and subsequently run atop the mysterious box of alarm detoxification that sits next to the register of this highly departmentalized department of the K'mon-n-Mart. And this department where Carroll now stands and pays for his tape is known as the Video Department and can be found easily from any point in this capacious store because it is on a platform two steps or one ramp above the rest of the store. And Carroll now owns a copy of "The Shy Man's Guide to Meeting Women," and as he descends the currently un-wheelchair-laden ramp of this platform he is given directions on how best to proceed to the Home Electronics Department, which lies across the vast expanse of the K'mon-n-Mart.

And now emboldened with said ownership as well as with the knowledge, gleaned from the small italics on the back of the box, that "The Shy Man's Guide to Meeting Women" runs a duration of only four and ten minutes, Carroll is blessed with a plan that is so divinely inspired it seems to emanate from the very fluorescent lighting far above him, from a source, in any case, to which the salesperson in Home Electronics would surely wish to defer propitiatingly. And when he arrives in Home Electronics there is indeed no clerk at the counter, that person being otherwise occupied at the joystick of a personal computer and relieved to be able to deal with Carroll by merely nodding without having even to divert his eyes from the more cogent invaders. And Carroll takes this as further confirmation that his mission is righteous and well guided as it has been from its inception at his home early this morning. And again it is so, for having never before operated such a device, his hand is swept about in the correct set of feather-touch commands on the face of the VCR demo unit, dancing lightly as if he had touched his first harp . . . and came there the music.

And the Home Electronics department of the K'mon-n-Mart comes alive with the image of the Concept Marketing logo blazing across four true and sturdy shelves of between nine and twelve television sets each. And follows there times forty-one a bursting of letters in all their sans-serifed glory: "The Shy Man's Guide to Meeting Women."

And all of these televisions produce sound in varying degrees. And what from some does emanate is every word of the tape. And what from others does emanate is the sibilance of our broadcast day: sssssssss.

And fourteen minutes commence.

And Carroll receives the word, sssssssss.

"Sylvia." This from the barmaid.

"Oh! Me?" This from Sylvia, black haired, small chested, and looking more like a wife than any dancer at *this* man's club (never mind that this man doesn't have a wife).

"Oh! Meee?" apes Carroll in a semi-audible falsetto.

Whatwasthat, thinks Sylvia, turning pretty damn quick from her position by the stage but seeing only that guy who's always in here. Nobody. Nothing. Her imagination.

Carroll draws a finger line down the side of his glass, and a drop of condensation clings to his skin. Round and ready to fall, that drop is under his mild inspection. Sylvia's ass ticks off toward the bar. Then a red conduit of light hits the mirrored ball above the stage, starting it on a slow rotation as if light really . . . well, mattered. The DJ/doorman lays down some patter, and Jasmine mounts the stage.

The men at the stage are numbers on the face of a clock. Jasmine always dances with order. She is the tiny luminous disk on the tip of the second hand. Carroll, sitting for the first time at the bar, has a slightly elevated viewpoint, and his feet search for atavistic clues re gaining purchase on the base of his barstool. Red splashes from the mirrored ball circle the stage lambently, like so many red-sweatered skaters in a rink. This is the flow that Jasmine takes, in a sense then spinning the room as she remains in place and entertains the visits of the men as they pass. She's good, really good, in a democratic sort of way, for the difference between her longest and shortest pauses in front of the men is merely seconds, if that. So she dances, to the confusion of her audience, with a statistician's disregard for the size of each man's tip as it dangles from the rail. Mr. If–you're-lucky-you'll-get-a-buck-when-you're-naked enjoys the same dose of her attention as Mr. Yes-boys-that-really-is-a-twenty-dollar-bill-in-front-of-me. Tick, tick around the stage. Jasmine doesn't care. To her it's X dollars per man, Y men per set,

Z sets per night. The current of the red lights rolls her out of a flowing body scarf and on to bachelor number N, where N is derived through an interpolation involving length-of-song, time elapsed, and the already assigned variable Y. Not to worry, N-1 (but we'll just call you Cashmere), she'll be comin' 'round again when she comes. Twice more.

"Lovelylady by the name of Jasmine, gentlemen. Jasmine will be right out for the second of three. While you're waiting, gentlemen, don't forget that all our lovelyladies are available for topless table dances. They're up close and personal, and if you'd like one they're all yours. Just ask your favorite lovelylady for details." Whine, two thumps, a needle scratches. "Okay, gentlemen, as promised with the second of three, put your hands together for the lovely . . . Jasmine." Some papers flutter over the closing mike, though from where he's sitting Carroll can see no papers being handled. The DJ/doorman returns to his chicken wings, picks up a plastic fork then puts it down. Never eat potato salad from a restaurant.

And as Jasmine, now two-thirds naked, retakes the stage, Stevie, who is killing time as well as her manicure in the dressing area, inquires of a dancer named Tamara, "So how come only days? Doesn't the money suck?"

"Quick," responds petite, strawberry-blond Tamara. "They're in for lunch, they're out." She goes back to nibbling a wayward thread from the folds of a costume. Then, as if the proper interval has passed, permitting the release of this additional information, she adds, "You don't get the ones that sit around for hours." She's said enough.

A thoughtful pause, then Stevie responds, "I guess I'm still too new here. I haven't noticed any of those."

Snap. The thread is broken, hopefully not too short, and Tamara rolls the fabric between her fingers. "Me neither, really. Working mostly days like I do I wouldn't know about here. I mean, this night shift is unusual for me. Highly unusual. But when I worked in Atlanta and it was *all* nights —I mean *only* nights—it got so they had to bounce guys out every now and then." She nods gravely: the straight dope. "You could count on it: some guy would practically be living in the place. Night after night, always trying to talk like he was everybody's brother, so's you couldn't even go near him for fear of making conversation. Yeah. There was one guy, I remember, the manager and the doorman had to tell him to leave cause he was harassing the girls." At this point Tamara looks to the floor beneath her pretty feet: the moral. "And he never once put his hand on any one of us."

"Atlanta, huh," says Stevie, unable to think of an actual response. Against her better judgment she gives trim to a tender cuticle.

"Every night till four ayem, sister. I made beaucoup bucks, too."

"Lots of money, huh." Ouch! Not wanting Tamara to see the blood, she wraps the finger in its own fist.

"I heard last night was your first night here. So how'd you like it?" Tamara wants to know. Finished with her costume, she folds her hands in her lap, finally ready to proceed with the interview.

Stevie smiles too widely, glances at the mirror. Yep, lipstick on the teeth. "Swell. Kind of loose at closing though—girls leaving early, last-minute favors and errands—that was new to me. I'm used to a little more structure." She extends her finger, using it like a toothbrush to remove the lipstick from her teeth.

A new tone here from Tamara: trying real hard to sound bored, as opposed to really being bored. "Oh? Where'd you used to work? Vegas?" And with this a jocular little chuckle.

"Yeah, right," laughs Stevie, waving off the notion with her hand and catching a glimpse of red in her peripheral vision.

Tamara joins her laughter only after she's sure it's safe. "Well, where then? Where'd you used to work?" And wanting to foster the nascent intimacy she thinks she felt in their shared sarcasm, she adds, "After Vegas, I mean," and the small joke is renewed.

"Please," says Stevie, still smiling but recovering appropriately from her laughter. "No, actually I was at the Playboy Club in Century City. I was a Bunny. That is, I was a Bunny until they shut the doors." Strange. She feels moisture on her finger.

"*You* were a Bunny?" says Tamara, smile smack-frozen in mid-disbelief, not sure if it's just more kidding. Or was this silly bitch really a Playboy Bunny! "But that place has been closed for a long time. What have you been doing?"

Stevie catches the tone, sees that she has divulged more than she should have, and turns her attention back to her fingers. That cuticle *is* bleeding. "Just temp work here and there. I had some money saved." Right. I'm just a hard-working-class waitress. Pennies for a rainy day, wouldn't want to have to sell the 308. What would go first, the Ferrari or its phone? Can't have one without the other.

"Temp work," demands Tamara: not good enough. "Like what, a secretary or something?"

These things sure bleed a lot, thinks Stevie, growing uncomfortable with the conversation not to mention bored. She can't remember the last time she *had* to work. She's not even sure what her rent is these days. Does she have to spell it out? "No. Reno. I did a couple of shows in Reno. I knew some people." Holding up her finger, she adds, "I'm bleeding."

But Tamara had already noticed that, and simply says, "Reno. Huh."

The music wanes. In comes Jasmine to prepare for the third of three, the last song of her set. "How are you guys holding up?" she asks cheerfully.

So under the guidance of the mirrored ball and the other sundry skylights the evening progresses. There are a lot of girls dancing tonight, and Carroll finds himself drinking a lot of sparkling apple cider at the bar, waiting for Stevie to do her sets. She is rarely working the floor tonight, not out here hustling table dances, preferring instead the getting-to-know-you gossip of the dressing area, or so Carroll guesses. He's seen that tack before in new girls, especially on overstaffed nights such as tonight. The manager is unwilling to say anything, for it might indicate to whomever he works for that his scheduling abilities are less than sterling, and he needs to hang on to the scheduling as a way to leverage the girls.

But when Stevie's out here, when she does do her sets . . . well, Carroll's attention is there and there only. Here she comes; he can feel it. He anticipates her introduction, knows the words a mike-knock ahead of the DJ/doorman: ". . . Stevie . . . Stevie . . . Stevie. . . . "

Then Stevie dances.

Then it's over—a twinkle—and Carroll discreetly wipes from his face what sweat he can with a cocktail napkin, orders another sparkling apple cider.

An idea has been growing in the back of his head. It's something he doesn't want to face, but it's there nonetheless, and given that he's been acting rashly lately, he knows that he won't ignore this thing forever, that he'll look at it, address it, assess it. He will, maybe not tonight, but probably tonight. He will.

"One more time, gentlemen, put your hands together for the lovely Stevie. Okay. . . . And up next—remember, gentlemen, that the lovely Stevie, as well as all our lovely-ladies, is available for a topless table dance. They're up close and personal, and the perfect way to have a private conversation with the lady of your choice. Just ask your favorite dancer for details. Okay, gentlemen, on we go with the first of three from the lovely . . . Nikki, gentlemen. Put your hands together for the lovely Nikki."

Nikki. Pretty blond hair, right? Still, Carroll looks to his left at the row of tiny curtained booths reserved for the table dances. There are four. Each is merely a small bench for the customer to sit on, curtains on either side providing the privacy, while the dancer leans into the booth from a standing position. Gyrating. Dipping. Panties on. Top off. Why? He can see two head-tops (toupees?) above the curtains, two dancers moving in front of those. Often a dancer will drop down for conversation, often keeping her hands on the higher woodwork, sort of like a gibbon. Talking. Why? Jasmine is doing that now, talking earnestly with some guy who's got too much hair and probably too much money. Hence the conversation, right?

From up here at the bar he can see quite a bit more of all this than he's used to seeing from his usual vantage points along the rail or around the general floor of the club. This chair is higher. Maybe not such a good thing, better to miss some of the sights. Stevie is already out of the dressing area, talking to a customer and gesturing to the booths. Last night he suffered sheer hell (and this was from a distance!) each time (three) he was forced to witness her dance so close, so out-of-his-sight, for some jerk who was so not-Carroll. Now . . . yes, she's walking over here with this guy. A size forty-six suit. An empty booth. Oh God. Yes, sparkling apple cider, that's fine, thank you.

For all his will to not look, Carroll's eyes keep drifting to Stevie and Size-Forty-Six like a tongue to a bad tooth. What he gets is her silken back and golden hair, pressing relentlessly close to the repugnant figure seated in the booth. Of course they can't be touching . . . and neither one is talking much. She *does* look a little bored. WHOA!!! She looks up, catches him staring. Back to cider, back to cider.

When you gonna ask her? When you gonna ask her?

Nikki is her usual acrobatically competent self, playing the gimmicks with casual finesse, keeping herself clean by never staying too long in any one mirror. The guys dig her, and the rail waxes green.

Whenyougonnaaskher? Whenyougonnaaskher?

He's not sure which dance this is for Nikki—the what of what? He's not even sure if he's ever before been unsure which dance any dancer has ever been on—the this of that. Lights, red, blue, looks-like-something-new, are everywhere. His cider bubbles more than it ought to. Less?

Nikki. Nikki. *Not all that blond, buddy.* What? What does that mean? What difference does that make? Either this is the same dance or Size-Forty-Six is dropping twenties all the fuck over the place behind that curtain. She's still at it. Stop! he wants to scream. He closes his lips over the straw that half floats in his drink.

"Stah!" he screams down the straw. But no one around him even hears, and cider bubbles up out of the very full glass and onto the bar.

WHENYOUGONNAASKHER?WHENYOUGONNAASK-HER?

She's still at it. Stop looking. She's still at it. He decides to tip Nikki. Since he is not seated at the rail, this necessitates standing and walking a few feet. Okay, no problem. She's still at it. Stop looking, he's not you. Tip Nikki. Carroll rises, stands in front of his barstool—no room to go anywhere else. There are numerous muttered excusemes between him and the relatively clear area behind the seats that surround the railing, each requires a minimum of one repetition. Bad stuff, sure enough, but at least it keeps his attention focused away from her (she's still at it). Wait. His change is on the bar. He left his fucking change on the bar, and all he has in his wallet are two twenties from his bank machine. How can he tip Nikki if his change is on the bar? Why is he standing here in everybody's way if he's not going to tip Nikki? He certainly can't afford to give her a twenty, but how can he walk back through the Gauntlet of Excuseme only to come out again? How can he go back and not return, having done nothing? Maybe the bathroom . . . yes, that's it, he's going to the bathroom. He starts walking across the floor to the door to the men's room. Wait. How can he go to the bathroom and leave his money sitting on the bar? There he stands, the light playing over his features foolishly (it's not his light, not for him). He suddenly realizes that the music is dying, Nikki is finished with this dance, the what of what. There may not be another. That option may be closed to him. Wait. There'll always be another dancer, so you'll always have the option to tip. Okay. No problem, that. He's left with how to go to the bathroom and leave his money sitting on the bar.

Then his eye is on Stevie, who is away from the booth and fastening her top, and Carroll sees the answer: just go. The situation is no longer in your hands, so just go.

And he does, and he comes out, and his hands are still damp from the electric hand-dryer, and Stevie is providentially standing right here (or somehow just standing right here where he never expected her to be standing) and he says, croaks really, like quick and without a thought, like a yelp after someone steps on your foot, "Dance . . . at table? Um . . . topless table?"

It's awfully quiet. He can hear his own heartbeat. He wonders what her expression is, but her face is about the last place he'll be looking right now.

Stevie sighs: *againnnnn?* She wonders what this guy is looking at on the floor, plans to check her shoes for gum while she's in the ladies' room. "You want a table dance?" she confirms.

"Yes," he says, nodding and now looking at her shoulder (shoulder?).

"Okay, they're twenty dollars per song. Okay?"

"Yes."

"Okay, great. Ahh . . . tell you what: why don't you go over there, and I'll be along in just a minute." A song has just started, so they'll have to wait for the next—these guys flip if they don't get their full song—and she really doesn't want to rap with this guy while they wait. She's got to go to the bathroom anyway. She'll just make sure she's out in time.

"Yes. Thank yOU," says Carroll a bit too loudly there on the end.

And boy does it sound strange to Stevie.

Before he even makes it back to his barstool he can see that his money is untouched. Only then does it occur to him that when he asked Stevie for a table dance (he asked Stevie for a table dance!) he really didn't know if he had the money to pay for it . . . no, wait: he's got two twenties in his wallet, and his change will be of no help here anyway (twenty dollars per song!). He must not have been thinking clearly because in the bathroom he prepared himself for the eventuality of having all his money stolen. That didn't happen, but retaining possession of a few dollars is small shelter from the storm of anxiety that is rapidly gathering in his gut. Nikki is still on the stage, doing what *must* be the third of three. Now he sits and waits for Stevie and feels real terror.

He casts to the left. There is only one booth in use, seems to be no one waiting. That's good; at least he won't feel so much like one out of four caged rats. . . . What the hell is this? He always feels like a caged rat, except during the incident today on the twelfth floor, the SoLo/Bombgate tiff. That almost felt good, like touching something nice that you've only been looking at up till then. What about Stevie? How could he feel like a rat (it's almost time!) sitting in front of her, talking to her? She'll be dipping for him. She'll be hanging from the woodwork to talk to him. Oh, God! What the fuck could he possibly have to say to her? Nothing. He is a rat. He knows. And in a minute or two she'll know it too. She'll know it forever and that'll be that. This is horrible (is the music getting softer?). It's still too crowded. He doesn't have time to make a clean getaway, and if he left now he could never come back. It's like being on the 405: the freeway is backing up fast; there's an exit RIGHT HERE, but you're in a center lane with no hope of getting over. He ran an errand to Long Beach once for work: get signatures, nobody else available, big emergency. Caught on the 405 for an extra hour coming back and he's sure everyone thought he spent that time on personal business. No one would talk to him, and to make matters worse, the next day they had to send someone else because the wording of the agreement was wrong. They gave him the news sarcastically, gauging his reaction, as if he already knew, as if it had been swapped out of his car by opposing counsel while he was busy jerking off in an adult bookstore somewhere.

"—lylady by the name of . . . Nikki, gentlemen. Next up is—"

"All set?"

She's RIGHT HERE. How did she get through the crowd so fast? They've parted, for chrissake. Of course. They would. She's so close, just here at the barstool, he can even smell her . . . well, he's not sure what it is, but it smells expensive. It smells like the green-smocked women behind the glass cases of the cosmetic departments in the mall. All a mystery. It smells exquisite. God! she's beautiful. All set.

"Are you ready? Because the song's about to start. If you still want a dance we'd better get you into a booth."

She's impatient, doesn't want to deal with this one at all. Maybe. . . . No. . . . Well? "If you're not ready we can do it later, or you could ask any of the other girls . . . if I'm not available . . . or if you changed your mind." C'mon, little guy, give me a clue.

"No, no, now. I mean, now's good. I'm ready. Here, I'll. . . . " He goes fishing for his wallet.

"Don't worry about that. We'll take care of that after. Let's just grab a booth before the music starts, okay?" She smiles, nodding, and sidesteps over to the first empty booth, hoping he'll follow.

He does, after an inertia-breaking moment, follow her magnet like a ball bearing. Things are moving very fast for him right now, but later he'll recall this moment and be amazed at the sense of liberation, at how he stood here, in Indiscretions, caring not one bit about who was looking at him, how he looked to them, or, for that matter, who or what was around him. The exception being, of course, Stevie, who now stands to the side of the booth, indicating, she hopes, that he should sit down on the bench. No problem, baby. He rolls right by her and drops into the pocket.

She lowers a small hinged counter over his knees, a potential barrier, no doubt, between dancer and excitable customer. Rules of the game, his feelings are not hurt. He hears a pounding in his ears, and it takes a moment to distinguish it from the drumbeat of the new song and the microphone taps of the DJ/doorman. A girl moves onto the stage in the background beyond Stevie. He doesn't know or care who it is. The music is now at full volume, and Stevie efficiently removes her top, placing it on the floor next to some other piece of fabric she was carrying around. Carroll's eyes drop, grateful for the little bundle to focus on at her feet. Indifferent to his apparent inattention, which she now recognizes as nervousness (aha! so that's it), she begins her dance as if his eyes were fixed on her breasts: a job to do. Okay, okay . . . Worth Doing Well:

"So what's your name?" she tries.

"Carroll Mine," he says a little breathlessly, hoping he gets this one right.

Left nipple justtt barelyyy missinggg his right eyelash, she drops to a squat with her arms on the small counter, not hanging from the booth in the conversational posture that he has so often witnessed in the other girls. He can't believe how close she's getting to him with her breasts, almost as if he were special, as if he and he alone were permitted to touch her. And this, the way she has her hands on the counter instead of above her on the woodwork, as if she really wants to talk to him and him alone.

"I'm Stevie," she says. "I've only been here a couple of days—actually this is only my second night—but I think I've seen you here before, right?" She stands, then puts her ass out, her head in, swaying to the music and letting her hair brush over his face so that he'll get a noseful of her conditioner; also, she needs to gather whatever it is he says in response.

But he only says, "I know." He's never smelled anything so beautiful. He'll never forget this. Something he should ask her, maybe so, maybe so, shouldn't ignore these things.

She shrugs inwardly. Fine. They're about halfway through the song, and she's convinced that he poses no threat. This is a guy who plays strictly by the rules. She can afford to get a little closer and give the poor thing his twenty dollars' worth, probably his lunch money for the week (why do they do it?). His head is up now, and he finally seems to be looking at least in the direction of her breasts. Good. She takes a hard and fast dive in, swooping both nipples by his lips. A millimeter. An expert. Christ, he looks like he's going to faint. Too much. She does it again, closer. There we go. She owns him now. They just turned the corner, and she's got him trained. It's a small game, really kind of silly, but she knows that a lot of girls do it. It's a point you reach in the dance, a point where you've got the guy . . . well, hooked, and (it is silly) you can make his head bob around any way you like. So Stevie bobs Carroll's head a couple of times to help the time pass. Left, up, right, down, left— Stop it now! When the hell is she gonna grow up?

Oblivious to her game, he thinks, No, no. This can't possibly go on with everybody, can it? No, I hardly think so. I think it's time to WAKE UP! because she likes YOU, and you're definitely being told something here, pal. You're being sent some kind of far-out message, just like the hot tub dream last night. Maybe so, maybe so, shouldn't ignore these things. Impure as it sounds he'd like to have an erection right now, probably will get one later on at home. But God he's terrified now, too scared to get hard, and certainly too scared to talk to her. Yikes! that was close. He hopes she's not expecting him to touch her or anything. Oh, and the hair, more hair. The smell, the skin.

Then Carroll realizes something is happening—or unhappening. There's the voice of the DJ/doorman, and the music is getting softer, fading out. Stevie is stepping back, away from the counter and bending to retrieve her little bundle. Over! No, it can't be over already!

Two twenties, there are two twenties in the wallet.

"Um . . . Stevmmmm (direct address predictably mumbled), if you had time I was hoping we could do another?" this all spoken to either her feet or the counter.

C'mon, what are ya gonna do, say no? Cause if that's the case, young lady, then you can just march your little bottom right on home. "Well sure," she says, with the prettiest little smile this side of Pahrump.

As the second song begins Carroll feels the comfort of experience, but not much. What he really feels is less terrified, slightly more able to attend to the here and now of this most fantastic experience. He watches her face, her breasts, her ass when she shows it to him, so very close as with the rest of her. They don't speak much, both now having given up on small talk. Maybe there's even an element of familiarity here, as in the quietly accepted pauses of a long conversation. No, it's okay. We don't have to talk. So the world simmers down to a background hum, the music barely an unobtrusive soundtrack. There's only him, her body closer than he's ever been to anyone before. Too much potential confusion, too many decisions, best to leave it all like this, a vision. As close as it gets, all the heat, the fragrance, leave it, please sir. Leave it now behind your eyes, a pre-memory, sir, please. . . .

Oh! but the hair again flitting all around his face, but the song (how much left?), but the voice he needs again to hear, but the what-will-come-after, but the nakedness, but the breath, so close she is it falls on his cheek, hot, turn your nose, catch it, catch it. . . . Well now, isn't that a gift!

Small mist from heaven, sweet redolence from the mouth of an . . .

"Are you an angel?" he blurts out.

Stevie, somewhat dismayed that conversation has resumed, can't quite hear him over the music but knows by his inflection that there's a question awaiting an answer. She pulls away to face him then turns sideways and passes a nipple over his cheek, almost miscalculating and touching his ear.

"What?" she says.

"Are you an angel?" Infinitely patient now, glad that he asked, bewitched, perhaps, he is.

Oh, jeeze! "You're funny," she says. When is this dog-of-a-song gonna end? Heavy metal. It's toooo loooonnnngggg, toooo loooonnnngggg. She shows him her ass, snaps some elastic.

You're asking it wrong, dummy! That's not like the dream. Remember the dream? Try again. He takes a short breath: oh yeah. "What are you?" he tries.

Half amused, she says, "Okay, I'm an angel," but she also glances over at the manager's door. No reason. Reflex.

"You're an angel?" says Carroll earnestly, following his own indelible dream-script.

She frowns despite herself. Tersely: "Yes." Toooo loooonnnngggg. More breast-in-your-face, albeit set off slightly more than before.

He now too wrapped up in the so-far flawless flow of their conversation to notice her slight retreat says, "Then I want to ask you something."

"Ask," she says probably a little too harshly. She can sense the music nearing its happy end. Heavy-fucking-metal. Ugh.

Well that doesn't sound quite right . . . but close enough. Now he too can sense the music ending; he senses it through her. He realizes his heart is pounding, realizes that he simply doesn't know just how real this is, realizes that this may be the single most important moment of his life. Guided, that's it, he feels guided.

"Will the meek inherit the earth?" he says, choking off a sob and feeling an honest-to-god tear on his cheek.

Wham wham wham . . . wham . . . WHAM! Heavy-fucking-sucking-metal. Finally. Stevie smiles good-naturedly as she bends to retrieve her clothes. No way did he say that. What did he say? Okay, who cares. He didn't ask for another song, so who cares. She makes a big show of putting her top back on: he is exactly the type that would dig that. Even if he does want another song, no go. She's got to . . . umm . . . help out in the dressing room. Yeah. She promised the girls that she'd help out in the dressing room—excuse me: dressing area. She remembers the interview when she walked into this place for the first time, way after the requisite dance in his face, Fatso looking at the paper to recall the name they'd agreed on just thirty seconds earlier: "Now, ah, Stevie. Nobody in this place has no dressing room, see? Don't let the girls tell you different. They know better. We all share a dressing AREA. It ain't a room, it's an area. See?" What the fuck time is it already?

That was then, and this song too is now over. Dressed, wellsortof, polite but To The Point, she could be a stewardess collecting for drinks. "Let's see. That was two songs, so that'll be forty dollars," she says, vaguely hoping he doesn't repeat whatever it was he asked cause it's plum gone out of her pretty head anyway.

Rudely awakened but not at all offended, Carroll's in awe of this woman. Just like the dream. The whole thing, even the end, was just like the dream. Mysterious ways. Oh God, she *is* an angel. He pays her, goes back to the bar after watching her float away, and almost orders a bottle of water before realizing that the money he left on the bar has vanished. He looks around at the men near him, but what's that gonna get him? He looks up at the barmaid, and to his chagrin she is looking right at him, her eyes weary, just wondering about the tip.

The manager walks her out to her car—not exactly her idea of a safe escort but at least a known quantity. Last night, her first night, she was able to avoid this and slip out on her own, but really, that wasn't wise. Anything can happen past the click of the back doorknob. Men will wait, she knows. Men will wait.

"Don't tell me," says the manager, stopping dead in his tracks, kicking up a little dust and using the opportunity to drop his arm across her chest. He puts a hand over his eyes in a mock clairvoyant routine. "Did Daddy buy us a wed Fewawi?"

Oh fuck, a wed Fewawi, a red Ferrari. She forgot about the 308; she'd rather this guy hadn't seen it. He peeks through his fingers at her, smiling with his eyes and doing a hopeless little dance step in the gravel. Stevie can see that this guy thinks of himself as a *comic*, probably tried or thinks he should try going professional, maybe on his own stage. Maybe that's what happened to the Lilac Club pictured on his office wall. It has in the picture the look of a mere memory, wherever or whatever it was. This guy's baggage, she knows, is all about deals, goes with the territory.

"It was a birthday gift," she says in a tone that she hopes is amiable. It would be easier if she were naked. *What birthday was that?*

"And how many birthdays does it take to get a gift like that?" he says like it's an old joke between old friends.

Son of a bitch. Her fingers mercifully touch metal in her purse. "Well thanks for the walk," she says, jingling her keys from her purse. "You were right. I feel much safer out here with you around."

Practiced, she's in the car before the issue of good-night even arises. Better to not even know what, if anything, his get-acquainted plan is. This is just one of the myriad reflexes that she has carried with her for years, that seemed to develop right along with her breasts (what came first?), like the quiver she can put on her lip. Crack the window, put him in the rearview mirror. He'll be back for more, thinks he already got something.

It's an easy jump onto the 405, and in no time she's home in Westwood. Her apartment is actually a condominium on Wilshire Boulevard, owned by one of her boyfriend's corporations and rented back to him (well, her, but he pays the rent) as a way to beef up a column entry on his Schedule Whatever each April-automatically-extended-to-August. They've been together long enough now for him to stop coming around on a regular basis. His wife, new kid, feds breathing down his neck about the thrift in Denver, out of town next week, kisses on the phone, paging his flight. Her: "That's fine. Just be sure to call before you drop in." Him: "What the hell is that supposed to mean?" She remembers wondering, Why did I say that? But this is water over the dam, and things have settled into a stasis of well-enough-left-alone. She's good at least through the next fiscal year and really couldn't care less about the eventuality of a reevaluation. It's not something that would matter much to her anyway. Her father always admonished her, a little girl, not to cry, not to sully her pretty face with needless tears. Now a swell condo, good advice, to be sure. The place sparkles like a hospital. That's right, cleaning day. She chose none of this furniture, never understood his explanation of how it came to be here, never heard of insured furniture before, furniture that gets photographed every six months. When she returned from Reno there was a note from these insurance men: *Understand you are on vacation. Had to let ourselves in and rephotograph sofa. You appear in previous photo. Our error. Sorry for intrusion.*

Stevie pings around the kitchen for a while, tossing down a cracker here, a swig from the milk carton there. She bites a pickle then puts it back in the jar, changes her mind, fishes it out, and drops it in the disposal. Such is dinner, and she dries her hands. Picking up her purse from the counter, she goes into her bedroom. Here she gets a (coincidentally) bank-style vinyl pouch from the bottom of her underwear drawer and adds to its already voluminous contents the money from her purse. Mixed in with these bills are the two twenties given her by Carroll after their table dance. But she doesn't think about him or his twenties as she tucks away the pouch, hasn't thought about him at all since he left her sight. Rather, she collects some things from the bathroom and lays them out on a towel spread over the foot of her bed. Sitting cross-legged, she

clicks on the bedroom Sony and goes to work on her manicure. Soon she needs more cotton to help soak up the
blood. Later the hurt from her fingers invades her dreams,
but she is not one to cry out in her sleep.

Muted; that is, on but without sound. He needs the silence
to help him concentrate, to wrest some hint of direction
from his rather eventful evening. But he can't bear just
leaving it off, so the television is muted. What now? "The
Shy Man's Guide to Meeting Women" doesn't seem to
apply in this case. What he learned there, watching it at
the K'mon-n-Mart today, is far away from what he needs
to know. Face it: the tape was a ripoff, a bill of goods, filled
with absurd situations, improbable conversations, long
filler sequences of women walking on the street, equivo-
cal advice, and dubious aphorisms ("A short skirt is short
work"; "You're in the pink with that second drink";
"Avoid long conversations. Talk only of your car or movies, never politics or books—she might not be a reader!
Why bend her ear when you can bend her over?"). In or
out, man. Everything that comes across that screen is an
absolute, every pixel on or off. Heaven or hell. That tape
simply doesn't wash. He wonders if it ever really did to
anybody, or was it always just a scam. The lesson here,
he grows surer by the minute, is that what needs to be
learned is already known, was in fact learned long ago,
and the trick is to find out where it is hidden within
himself.

Peripherally he picks up a light dancing in the shadows of the room. There, he feels it: a tiny temblor is jiggling the ceiling fixture, but it's over practically before it
begins, not even time to dash for a doorframe. Hell, he

doesn't even have the inclination to dash for a doorframe. There are angels in this world, and earthquakes are now out of his hands. Just like the dream, he thinks, it was so close, I can't ignore it. This is the closest he's ever been to what they call religion (though he isn't calling it that). Another rumble, small aftershock. They'll probably say on the news tomorrow that both of these are aftershocks to some bigger quake of months ago and miles away. Maybe these are big quakes in some far-flung corner of LA. In any case the last one set off a car alarm down in the garage. There's another one, sounds like on Hawthorne, probably that guy's BMW, that guy who's out there every Saturday with one of those car-washing wands that they advertise on TV. No quiet. Still no fear.

So what's his plan? What's his hurry? After all, he did meet her, right? Maybe that tape wasn't so useless. Chock-full, it could have been, of subliminal messages; hours later, he meets her. Still he needs a plan. It all seems too little, too late. Time itself has taken on an importance that he never felt before Stevie, and this is silly. He knows well enough that he has no relationship with this woman. Now now, don't sell it short. She was nice to him tonight, nicer than the rest of the world is to him. She was missing the nasty little element of conspiracy that he sees behind so many eyes, so many doors. Always on his mind, there are so many ways to go wrong. It does matter, and it matters now. He's got to talk with her, got to have her talk back, and without a twenty-dollar meter ticking away between them, even without those sublime breasts between them. Well, covered . . . out of his face . . . for a while, anyway. This is serious. This is an angel. She's here to tell him something. He's got to listen.

The car alarms have either shut off or passed into the vast WhoCares of the Hollywood din. Carroll falls asleep, has a bizarre dream about Stevie driving him to her home: she lives in a bomb shelter, and when she excuses herself to bathe and shave her back (?) he spots the missing SoLo/ Bombgate file, mostly hidden under a stack of old *TV Guides*. He tries to grab the file, but he hears her coming back and stops. "How do you remember to smile," he asks her when she returns, smiling, to the room.

Fridaysaturday

Good under pressure, he realizes of Pam. Without jeopardizing their buddyship she's trying to make clear to him the urgency of locating the SoLo/ Bombgate file.

"We have *got* to find this thing pronto." This in a half-whisper though her boss's door is closed and there is no one around to hear.

Once again Carroll has been waylaid on his way from the elevator to his desk. Once again SoLo/Bombgate has turned out to be the First Thing In The Morning. In fact Pam herself is still wearing her trenchcoat, a New York habit she refuses to give up no matter how perfect the

Southern California climate is, dammit. Fair enough, it adds to the element of conspiracy she seems to be seeking, so much so that for a paranoid instant he wonders if she purposely kept it on while waiting for him. But then he notices that she's still holding her lunch, a microwaveable container filled with red stuff, so she must have just walked in.

She continues, leaning closer and deepening her whisper. "That file has original documents in it. (pause for effect, profound nod) The client is coming in on Monday afternoon, and if we don't come up with that file it'll be both our (and the most intensely whispery whisper yet) *asses!*"

Carroll knows whose ass it'll really be: Pam's boss, the litigation attorney who's working on the case and who will be meeting with the client Monday afternoon. This guy is an associate, so he poses no real career threat to anybody but himself; both Pam and Carroll know this, but he would never dare mention it to her; that's not who he is. Was there anything about yesterday's encounter that he should tell her? Has she already heard about it?

"I tried upstairs yesterday."

"I heard."

Was this a test? He's not sure what to say now. Realizing his finger is still stupidly gesturing up, he blushes and looks down. Is that a blue thing in her red stuff?

"Carroll," she says, "I think that might be a dead end. Look, we all make mistakes—you least of all, but you are human. Maybe we should consider the possibility that the file was simply misplaced in the wrong drawer. Lord knows I've done that, and I don't handle nearly as many files as you do. It's okay, all we have to do is find it and everything will be perfect." She sighs and squints:

brainstorming, cooking up a plan. "I don't know. Maybe the best thing would be a drawer-to-drawer search of the file room, then a cubicle-to-cubicle search of the secretaries, and finally an office-to-office search of the attorneys. What do you think?"

What does he think? What does he think? He thinks he knows exactly where that fucking file is. That's what he thinks. *I've never misplaced a fucking file in my life!*

"That must be it," he says (that is a blue thing). "I'll start first thing. I'll let you know how it's going before lunch." He shuffles in place, a habit that he'd like to lose but that seems entirely appropriate right now.

"I knew I could count on you. You're a lifesaver." She indicates with an outstretched finger her boss's door. "And don't think HE doesn't appreciate it too." Here she smiles tightly, lips plump and pursed like two greasy red-brown doggy treats.

He walks away wanting to puke. Maybe it's the blue thing in her red stuff. He'll find SoLo/Bombgate all right. He'll find it.

At his desk there has appeared over night a memo from the office manager outlining a new numbering system that is being considered by the Executive Committee for possible implementation as early as next month. Said system, the memo goes on to explain, would be initially applied exclusively to the relatively small entertainment department, its efficacy there to be used in an ultimate determination of whether to adopt it firm wide. To facilitate the ordering process for the vendor, as well as to commence what will become a weekly tracking procedure of all entertainment files, would Carroll please update that department's inventory, file contents and current location,

no later than three days prior to the next Executive Committee meeting. He rereads the memo, puts it down, picks
it up and reads it again. Entertainment is indeed small, so
small in fact that the department itself handles and stores
all its active files and he hardly knows what's up there.
In theory, of course, he is presumed to be right on top of
every file jacket in the firm, where it is, what's in it—call
'em off the top of his head, instant recall: *you're a lifesaver.*
In practice he handles mostly litigation. That department
being the largest and tending to have several attorneys
working on the various ancillary actions and cross com-
plaints of a single case, they need a nexus for their files, a
reliable yet expendable scapegoat. The other departments
seem to know this and generally leave him alone, handling
their own work, only occasionally sending down a hoary
old stuffed-to-splitting jacket for shipment to the archives
or requesting a new file number and jacket, labeled, stapled,
creased, and cross-referenced in an always out-of-date
card file on Carroll's desk. This memo is asking for at least
twenty hours of work. Normally he would jump on it just
to get it off his desk and to keep it out of his dreams. But
it seems puny compared to Solo, and he feels fortunate
that they're breathing down his neck about finding the
latter; it'll make for a good excuse should the office manager bust him for not plunging into this silly-ass entertainment inventory.

Drawing off a long sticky string of Highland (really
made by Scotch) Magic 810, he's about to tape the memo
to the top of his desk for safekeeping when he gets an idea.
Entertainment is on twelve. Pam's advice notwithstanding, so is SoLo/Bombgate. In fact the fat fuck's office is at
the same end of the hall. The more Carroll thinks about

this the better it sounds. Hell, it's likely that the corporate clown has some entertainment files on his off-limits credenza. A lot of the partners muscle their way into these matters to meet some future falling star of a celebrity, or just to get their initials added to the routing slips of the firm's entertainment subscriptions, the *trades*. Carroll's almost sure he heard this guy in the elevator one day crowing over his lunch at Jimmy's with Ed McMahon. McMahon's been in the office before—Carroll's seen him— so he might well be an entertainment client. Who knows. Either way, this memo would work fine. It's a one-stone way to hang around on twelve all day. It's a passport back into that office. It's a way to get his nose in that credenza. Excited now, he puts the memo in the back of his inventory clipboard and carefully winds the pulled–out tape back onto its roll.

Strong of mission, he ascends the special company staircase, which the firm was finally permitted to construct only after leasing one hundred percent of the square footage on both floors, eleven and twelve, late last year. A massive wooden winding affair and long yearned for since the ticky-tacky elevators revealed their propensity for downtime, as well as should-have-been-downtime, the prestigious trick of building it was managed, evidently, through some back-room negotiating involving the brusque building manager who sported short sleeves and military tattoos, and the comically skittish owner of the strange import company that was very comfortable on twelve with one little corner suite and only two years down on a five-year lease. Carroll got this much because the next day he was offered overtime to help the import guy move out over the weekend. It was one of the few times he's ever been comfortable with a stranger, but though they hit it off from opposite ends of mysterious corrugated cartons, Carroll never got the details of the meeting or why the guy was clearing out, only dots and dashes of tight-lipped yet oddly wry advice about vegetarianism and sex with two women. Everybody had the idea that this guy had been somehow muscled out, but after moving day, Carroll couldn't shake the notion that the firm and the building had played right into his hands. Carroll still has his tip, one of those wicker finger traps; when they parted the guy put it in his hand like a palmed twenty, only better.

Twelve is gearing up for battle. The people up here fancy themselves an elite force, lots of hard, intense work followed by lots of hard, intense play. Sipping their coffee as they run down the hall, cradling phones while rifling through files, sometimes two phones, even a headset on one girl, sweat, success, going-for-it–ness, car phones, vanity plates that spell out stuff like STAR LAW, assertiveness training, business class then first class, greased palms and last-minute reservations at four different restaurants for the same time just-in-case-we-change-our-minds, watches and cars and houses disguised as life's rewards because they can't come up with any better ideas, because it's the best they can do anyway and they know it. Work hard, play hard. The whole lot of them make Carroll wonder what the point is. He's an insect to them, and this is one of the few things he likes about himself. They also keep most of the chiefs-of-staff up here, torpid old partners like the corporate fuck who's sitting on Solo. Strategically dilatory, especially in contrast to the urgency surrounding them, these guys are either holed up in their offices or ambling about the floor, grunting each other's name should they pass, dropping in a low voice some wry conspiracy, a dollar figure or a date, like some great cholesterol-driven amorphous brain trust. Maybe they're on display here as motivation for the minions, something to either fight for or aspire to. Carroll just wishes the place were empty so he could get on with his job. Even at night—two, three in the morning—there's always some jerk up here reviewing a contract or drafting a brief. Only once was Carroll up here alone, last year when the newly constructed staircase was being varnished. Some sort of ventilation problem caused a secretary to faint, and they evacuated the office for a few hours. On the sidewalk with sirens in the distance, Carroll was surreptitiously sent back up to twelve at the bidding of an entertainment associate who, remembering that there were pay phones in the garage, pined for his Rolodex. His secretary was simultaneously dispatched to the savings and loan in the lobby for rolls of silver—an insult there somewhere—while her boss nervously quipped to an onlooking partner that the phone change would be billed off to Julio Iglesias . . . or was it Prince?

Today the plan is to lie low, spend the morning in the secretarial bays actually working on the entertainment inventory. This way he will establish a presence on the floor to add to his credibility should he get busted snooping during lunch. He'll also keep the memo handy for just such an emergency. His *papers.*

So it goes. Throughout the morning he makes a big show of peering into overstuffed file drawers, consulting his clipboard, and making notes. By eleven o'clock he has worked his way around the corner and as near as possible to the SoLo/Bombgate file. He's listing entertainment files stacked on the floor of the empty secretarial bay next to Mr. My-office-is-hallowed-ground's secretary, Beth Minnery (known predictably behind her back as Misery). Ninety-six pounds, alabaster white in complexion, been with the firm a villion years, Beth's your basic harmless nightmare who thinks she's got a line on the same brand of power and truculence found in your basic not-so-harmless terrorist group. She is nervously seated at her desk, typewriter covered, her purse before her, poised for takeoff. Though it's only just after eleven, she likes to be ready from now to eleven-thirty, avoiding any long-term commitments, like say typing a letter. About this time each day she grows anxious, afraid that her boss's door will open and she'll be given something to do, something urgent that would infringe on her lunch time. But provided that doesn't happen she will, as she has done for as long as anyone can remember, disappear in her 1966 Oldsmobile Cutlass from eleven-thirty to one-thirty. No one knows where she goes, what she does. Two-hour lunch. Every day. Carroll, in line with the common wisdom, assumes they give her this as a way to give her nothing else.

"Young man, we have some boxes over there. I hope you're not picking through our boxes," she challenges Carroll from over the partition. Evidently she has decided that this would be a safe way to eat up a few minutes without risking a long-term conversational commitment.

Carroll decides to scare her off. "I was about to come see you about that, Miss Minnery. I have an inventory to do here, and wonder if you could maybe help me out with your files. I know you're busy, but it should only take twenty or thirty minutes."

Silence. Then flustered rustling. "I have an appointment for lunch. . . . I'm much too busy today. . . . Isn't that *your* job? My time is far too valuable to be spent helping the support staff. . . . Couldn't you work it out while I'm gone so you're not in my way next week?"

He hears her getting ready to bolt. He impulsively decides to take a chance and press it. Informing Misery that he'll be in her boss's office would really cover his ass. "Umm, okay. I was told to list everything asap, so I hope you'll have time to at least peek into HIS office before your appointment."

Suddenly she is before him, purse on arm, a well-monitored Timex strapped around the other, worn way up on the forearm, almost to the elbow. She looks about to burst under the pressure of this unexpected quandary. For a moment he thinks he blew it, of course *she* would know the history, would have been told to keep him out of HIS office at all costs. He should have stuck with the original plan of lunchtime snooping. But no, she's too wrapped up in her getaway.

"I'm afraid you're on your own," she says, gaining resolution as she speaks. "HE's already left for a long weekend. And I'll be taking off the afternoon." She pauses before committing, but a glance at her watch opens this final gate. "You'll simply have to work it out yourself. And don't make a mess!" And she huffs off down the hall before he can even thank her.

It is a Friday; lunch is of a greater concern than it would be on any em through tee-aich, and in no time the twelfth floor is real quiet. Sweating under the collar despite all the green lights, Carroll slips stealthily into the office. It seems even more disorganized than before. He was only in here for a minute the last time, but he could swear that there are even more files strewn about. An entire shelf's worth is lined up on the brown leather sofa though the credenza looks as overloaded as before. Maybe he's just seeing more this time because he knows he's got more time to look. In fact, there's quite a lot of goofy stuff in this office: the usual corporate awards, framed certificates commemorating stock issues, Lucite cubes flanked by gold Cross penpencils and bearing an imprisoned microchip; turn-of-the-century pen-and-ink caricatures of sideburned solicitors and beer-bellied barristers holding fast in meretricious frames; four different briefcases (for a guy who hasn't carried anything away from his office in twenty years); three umbrellas for the relentless Southern California rain. . . . What's this? A small photograph under the glass desk top, and it's too much: there he is, the fat fuck himself, looking fatter and older than ever, and seated, face all red and self-satisfied, between two gorgeous women. They're barely dressed, panties and bras. This must be from some repugnant old-guy stag party or something. These girls have got to be hookers, cause the jerk has his arms all the way around their backs, one hand firmly planted on each outside breast. Unbelievable. Guess when you get that old you can touch anything you want. Carroll shakes his head, dumps his clipboard on the desk (over the photo), and once again scopes this fucker's credenza in search of the elusive SoLo/Bombgate file.

There he stays throughout the lunch hour, working the credenza. File after file, shelf after shelf, some packed so tightly that he has to struggle to pry apart the corners of the file jackets for a glimpse of the name, he works, driven. The afternoon commences, and he dashes downstairs to check for messages and to mark himself out and in for lunch; they'll get suspicious if they see he didn't take that lunch. He even goes so far as to make the IN time show him as five minutes late, a touch of authenticity and a nice touch at that, despite the fact that this then will be the first time he has ever returned late from lunch—a nice touch of irony, as well.

There is one message on his desk. Pam wants to know how the search is going. No she doesn't, he thinks as he scratches her an interoffice note: *Making progress—will keep you posted.* Goodnuff. He runs back upstairs, two steps at a time. He's invigorated by the search. It seems the most meaningful thing he's ever done at the firm. Maybe it's the autonomy of it, the way he can use them against themselves to satisfy their own request. He's the clockmaker. . . . No, that's not it. . . . He's an evil genius. . . . No, that's not right either. It's just that he needs to find this file, okay? Find the fucking file. Don't worry about why. Don't consider all the ways and reasons you have to never find it. Just find it. And, of course, don't ever never ever never think about where you'll be left once it's found. Best look for it. That's it. Look for it for all you're worth. By sweet George! How long it takes. How he longs to see this file. He really wants to win this. Shadows longer. Credenza down. Sofa.

But as with the credenza, and as Carroll works into the dark and into the stacks behind the door, into Misery's bay, the adjoining bay, into places where nothing of any use to anyone is ever kept, into desperation, it is obvious that Solo is Not Here. Late is the day, now, to him, but not over; this word is given him in one of those divinely maddening sparks that serve as flashes of motivation like so many coupons in the middle of the Wednesday newspaper. He's driven to the point of temporary abandonment, but only because it's a way to ensure resumption. Solo may not be on this floor—that much can be admitted. Solo may not be anywhere—shh! don't say that yet.

The restaurant is not exactly jumping. In fact they have the place to themselves, Stevie and her boyfriend. Around them waiters wipe silver and position water glasses, chef (cook) glares through his porthole unseen and returns to the early entrees. Stevie's boyfriend snaps his fingers and drinks are mixed at the bar. Nothing he could do. His wife needs dinner too, and if this is a little early, so what? Stevie should be glad for any time they can share. It's catch as catch can, one of the liabilities of an extramarital affair; she knows that as well as he does. If she wants to sit there and pout after he went to all this trouble to make it as nice as possible under the circumstances and got his Industry buddy who owns the place to open up early or at least to slip them in for an early bite as a favor and never mind that it's only about the most expensive fucking place on the west side and even this little time was hell for him to arrange on the homefront and that apartment doesn't come cheap either. . . . If she wants to sit there and pout WELL FUCK HER! And he wasn't gonna mention it but why the hell not who knows how much that carpet cleaning will cost . . .

"I came by the condo the other day. You weren't around—which is fine, you've got your own life, and I'm sure you were only out shopping or something—so I let myself in—"

"You let yourself in?" interrupts Stevie, trying to sound angrier than she is. She plays it mostly from memory.

She would have been very angry at one time, but now she really couldn't care less. He'll never notice the difference, and he wouldn't accept it if he did.

"Why the fuck shouldn't I?" he says, rolling with it yet holding back the *I pay the rent*, though she hears it just the same.

She looks down, resolutely straightens the napkin in her lap for the twentieth time since she put it there but does not remove it. "Maybe it's time I thought about moving," she says.

Swell. Here we go. He decides to bring it down a notch, to circumvent this too-familiar argument. "Look," he begins, slowly fanning the air with his palms pushing down on either side of his plate: *take it eeeeazzzzy.* "I'm sorry. You're right, and I won't ever use my key (which he paid for) again. Now, if that's settled, what I wanted to mention was the footprints on the carpeting." He pauses; they couldn't possibly have had *this* conversation before, yet it too sounds familiar, like deja vu, like he knows she'll speak here.

Oh! This is classic! Footprints on the carpeting? "Footprints on the carpeting?" she says incredulously. "Huh?"

Patiently: "Yes, there were white powder footprints all over the place. You must be putting baby powder on your feet and then walking around." A sip of water here to underscore this revelation, this inductive gem.

"So what?" she wants to know.

Fine. He'll tell her. "That carpeting cost a fortune, and there's no reason that you can't be a little more careful. Couldn't you wait until you're ready to put on your shoes before using the powder . . . or make sure that you stay in the bathroom until you're ready to put on your shoes . . . or—"

"No," she says simply. "No. I can't do any of that, and I can't tell you why. The carpeting will just have to be replaced every six months, okay?" She adds, "Call it a hidden expense," immediately regretting it for her own sake.

Entrees are coming. Time to calm her down. "Whatever. (more fanning) But you should know that I have people coming to clean it. They'll be there next Wednesday morning. I told them to call first, but don't worry about waiting around because I've informed the building manager and he'll let them in." And, using a tool he learned from his father, he puts his palms together and cleaves the air in front of him: That's that.

Oh looky! Here comes eighty bucks' worth of food to go with this great conversation. Time to chill out. "I'll try to be more careful," she says with a tired old trace of hollow supplication. Food. It's about time. It's a good thing she called the club and told them she'd be late. That filet sure looks overdone.

Customers, albeit early ones, are beginning to filter in past the red-vested prurient Latin valet and the weighty iron door that is normally the easiest part of getting into this place. Late evening will find a solicitous queue of hapless, weary couples outside this door, waiting for a table that will never come. But at this early hour anything goes, and people wishing to say that they have been here get their chance. A few tables are sacrificed for an hour or so, warmup for the staff, and the eager diners try hard to look unaffected, to breeze by the italic price column on the menu. The Lemon Pepper Pasta does well at this hour.

The eye of Stevie's boyfriend is caught by a fetching young girl who quickly looks down at her menu and places her hand on the outstretched arm of her companion. Wearing her finest yet still glaringly inadequate dress, she has a certain naivete that appeals to Stevie's boyfriend, who likes to think of such girls as blank canvasses (though this man is not a painter). He has slept with enough of these girls to know: this girl would never forget him. See how she pretends to be unaware of his gaze? He giggles inwardly at this. Now she scratches her nose as if it itches, and he thinks how he would like to smell her breath. Those first moments, when you're getting to know her body up close, all the little freckles, hair follicles, the smell of her armpits and the breath that comes out of her nostrils when you kiss too long. Nothing is bad then. She can do no wrong. Now she raises an eyebrow, and it makes her look precocious. But still, he would enjoy her at first, licking, maybe, tasting. Behind her ears. Swallow her spit. Panties. Flowery pictures on the panties, maybe drawings of those little cartoon girls with enormous hats like in the pictures painted on his daughter's bed.

Stevie decides to pick at her filet mignon (thirty-five dollars) and grab something on the way to work. Late is late. This'll really push his buttons, and she wishes she had ordered an appetizer so that she could not eat that as well. Of course if she wants to get him still madder she can tell him about the pool last Saturday. He'd flip out if he knew she spied on his kids, even if it was just once. Easy to find them: "Gotta go, gotta drive the kids to the pool." She beat them there with time to spare because he still had to get home from his morning workout. She parked down the street behind a Taco Bell and walked to the bleachers at the side of the fenced-in public pool. Sure enough he pulled up in front, kids out, forgot your towel, back, out again, pulled away, and he couldn't possibly have seen her, and she spotted the kids (just like their pictures), and from the other side of the chain-link fence watched them swim for almost two hours. Big deal. Even if they noticed her they would have no way of knowing who she was, what significance she had in their lives (zero). She remembers feeling transported in place and time to public pools of her own childhood. Chlorine, benign and ubiquitous, hung tough against the meaningless pre- and after-swim showers. Everybody smelled like the pool all summer. Beach towels laid out on hot, wet concrete. A little older and the lifeguards were so dreamy. How would they look to her now, those same guys? But back then, so dreamy, high above her and her friends, they sat. White stuff on their noses. Look up, hard to see them looming in the sun's glare. Get in trouble and have to sit at their feet. Get to sit at their feet.

Late Friday night, almost nine, back at his desk and the place feels deserted. Part of him wants to panic about being late for Indiscretions, and he tries to focus on that part as a way to decompress from the day's fruitless and frantic search. As much time as he spends at that club, you'd think he'd get sick of it, but the truth is he hates to miss it, any of it, like the way the White House must have guys monitoring all the news broadcasts all the time: it's not so much that they want to see everything as it is that they don't want to miss anything. He'll get there—it's Friday and they'll be packed till closing—he'll get there. The fluorescent bank overhead is only half on, every other tube, and it still seems way too bright. The thick plate-glass sheets of the windows have become dark mirrors as the interior light turns tail and runs from the eleventh-story darkness outside. He considers dropping another note to Pam, keeping her apprised should she get in early Monday morning. This, though certainly a prudent move, seems suddenly too much an invasion, and he fails to reach for a pen, and Solo crawls that much deeper into his heart. It feeds there, like a virus, and whimpers along with the sizzling protest of the fluorescent tubes as he hits the switch and makes his way down to the garage.

Traffic is benign, perky even. People driving on Friday evenings are generally happy about their destinations. He passes only one small accident, intersectional but without injury, guy in a suit being field tested on the curb. Carroll has never driven drunk, never even been drunk for that matter, but he knows it must be wrong. Still, it's strange to see a guy in a suit being busted for anything.

Indiscretions is predictably packed, and his late arrival forces him to park way in the back, at the end of a dark alley behind the adjoining gas station. He's only parked here once before, and though nothing happened to his car that time he still walks back through the lot to check on it twice after almost entering the club, captivated by virtue of its NO IN AND OUT PRIVILEGES sign if by nothing else. Inside is crowded as well. But men are flowing out as quickly as new ones come in, and it isn't long before Carroll is able to slip into a seat at the stage and set about scanning for Stevie.

He's been so preoccupied with Solo that he hasn't really thought about what he hopes to accomplish here tonight. Not that there's ever any question of not coming, but somehow he felt that finding Solo would be a source of enlightenment, a victory that she would see in his eyes. He was—still is—seduced by this opportunity, however improbable, to connect the two disparate elements in his life, like a wall socket and a desk lamp: connect them and suddenly they both have new meaning. It's not too late. Solo's still out there, and if he can get his hands on it, if he can have this search to show Stevie then maybe she'll be interested and make him glad that he bothered. She could know this about him, and his life wouldn't be a waste; rather, she'd reinfect him with her interest. Validate his day and make him that much more interesting. Perpetual motion. She and that file snagged him at about the same time. She would be an impossible dream if it weren't for the real dream he had about her. Solo should be in his hands by now, and the harder it is to find the more he wants to find it. Like it's a safer bet, reliable in its elusiveness.

The cocktail waitress, looking vaguely familiar, is busy enough catching up at the bar that he won't be reached for a while. He automatically puts a dollar on the rail, and only then does he notice Sylvia dancing (looks to be about the second of three) in front of him (she really does look like somebody's wife). Glancing over, he sees the four curtained booths are all occupied. Melissa, Tina, some new redhead, and Jasmine are entertaining the usual dreadfuls. As Tina bends way over to show a guy her ass, Carroll notices the guy's clothes. If that suit is any indication this guy must spend a fortune on clothes . . . and pressing. He's seen clients dressed like that at the firm. Like it wouldn't be enough to merely buy the suit, you'd also need somebody to put it on you each morning. No

Stevie there and this is best, better than dealing with the stress of again watching her alone with one of these guys. It did say on "The Shy Man's Guide to Meeting Women" that "clothes make not only the man, but the number of stories he's got to tell the boys at work the next day!" Carroll, though not all that interested in telling stories to the boys, does have to admit that he's never seen a girl like Stevie among the women who give wifely advice through the plywood doors of the dressing stalls in the men's department at K'mon-n-Mart. He should look into this tomorrow—what the heck, it couldn't hurt. He should find out where to buy expensive clothes and then go buy some.

He's getting thirsty, could use a sparkling apple cider. Still no Stevie, meaning she's probably gabbing in the dressing area. He can't really see the whole room, crowded as it is, so she might be anywhere. Sabrina, talking to a guy on the opposite side of the stage, looks up and catches his wandering eye. It hits them both like a shot, and for no reason they both look away too quickly. No. Stevie's definitely in the dressing area; she's not out here. Nothing to do but wait. He's beginning to feel empty. Maybe it would be okay if she did a table dance; at least he'd know where she is. He's really ready for a cider.

And then the waitress comes. Then Candy is on the stage. Dollars feed the rail. Ciders come and go. With a pang of denial he tells himself that it's simply a mistake in the rotation and that Stevie will be on stage right after Sylvia, now on her second set since his arrival. But he knows better. He knows, really knows in his gut that she's not here tonight. So what? She gets a night off just like anybody else . . . but *tonight*? Why is she not here just when he needs her most? Solo seems so very insignificant in the face of her absence. Still, he'd give anything to have found it. He feels empty here, convinced that she's not around. Maybe a good reason to return to work and keep looking, though he knows he couldn't leave here tonight, not until closing. Sparkling apple cider. He misses his television. No one home. Is she forever gone? Is she dead? Sparkling apple cider. She could come in late. She could come in tomorrow. She could have tomorrow off, too. Is it possible to never touch the things you really need to hold? What an enormous leap of faith it must have been for primitive men to value fire despite its intangibility. Is he missing this lesson? Did it get dropped from his personal evolution package, like the guys with hair on their backs and one big eyebrow, or the girls who can move their coccyx like a tail wagging under their skin? He misses his TV. Sit and wait. Come back tomorrow. Sit and wait.

The DJ/doorman stumbles through a few moments. A buzz, naked women, cider, men in suits, he hears "Stevie." He hears "for Stevie, gentlemen." He hears ". . . together for the lovely Stevie. . . ." And when she takes the stage he remembers hearing ". . . first set of the night . . ." and ". . . better late than never. . . ." To see her, to feel the flood of relief, he regains a little humor, and he at last remembers hearing ". . . direct to you from the bedside of her ailing grandmother . . . says she needs prescription money, gentlemen." For this a chuckle, a footnote to the laughter that died shortly after the joke was delivered (that must have been about when he heard it). Funny, he thought, how they're laughing like that.

This is the first time he's been seated at the stage during one of her sets. Well he might be at the stage, but it's still pretty damn crowded tonight, and it's doubtful that he'll be able to get much attention from her. Still, she hovers about as if he were the center, flitting left and right with a delicacy befitting the angel that she is. He looks about. Already dollars line the rail. He realizes that he's been so wrapped up in anxiety that he forgot to put his up, and red-faced, he hurriedly does so. Stevie dips, swinging a nod of her ass to him as well as to the man next to him and moving down the line. Carroll notices that the man puts up two more dollars. He has much experience here at Indiscretions, and normally he doesn't let big tippers intimidate him. On the other hand he is in hot pursuit of something. Old rules of conduct must be reevaluated on a daily basis, like him sneaking into Corporate Fatso's office. Decisively he pulls back his single, replacing it with a fin, and thus garnering the respect of at least one guy across the stage, whom Carroll catches reevaluating his own single after spotting the five. Stevie may not catch it until her second song, for she is pacing herself around the stage tonight (been watching Jasmine) and will likely end up near the curtain just as each song fades out. But catch it she will, and if she wants to keep within club policy she'll have to come back to him after her dance and whisper thankyou into his ear. He's actually seen guys get a little peck on the cheek during these thank-yous. But that wasn't Stevie, and it's a bit early in the game to be expecting stuff like that, and he'd better make sure he paces himself as carefully as she. Good, she, familiar on this new-to-her stage. So good. They're in this new territory together.

As Stevie disappears behind the curtain for her costume change, Carroll sizes up the guy who noticed his five-dollar bill on the rail. He's nervously looking around the room (probably never been here before), and Carroll is amused to see that he's added another single to the one he already had out. Well, he'll learn. He'll learn. What's he wearing? Looks like he spent a little money on those clothes, Carroll guesses, maybe not a lot, but a little more than Carroll spends. Sort of—what is that, green? light green?—sort of a light green shirt with black curlicues all over it. Can't see the pants, but it's an okay shirt. It's not a bad shirt . . . better than the striped thing that Carroll's got on, sent by his aunt from Houston last Christmas and complete with ersatz epaulets.

Sputtering microphone overtakes building music: "Here she is, gentlemen, for the second of three . . . Stevie, lovelylady by the name of Stevie."

Hmmm. She's changed into some sort of sequin costume. No place for curlicues on that thing. Carroll decides it must be new, or from some other job before. . . . Hold the phone! He never thought about it, but she must have worked someplace before here. Strange that he hadn't considered that before now, and he's suddenly overtaken with curiosity. A bit of regret too, that he talked only of himself during his table dance, never thought to ask about her. Maybe he is just like other men, the way they're portrayed by women on daytime talk shows he's seen on holidays and sick days. Always talking about themselves, these women complain of men. Men only want to talk about themselves. He saw a girl say this on "The Love Connection" once and thought her date, pictured in the little corner box, was gonna die with embarrassment. "How was dinner?" Chuck had asked her. "Great," she answered, "if you've got nothing better to do than hear his life story" (or something like that). Though he felt bad for the guy at the time, Carroll made a mental note to never talk about himself to a woman. Guess he forgot. He's like all the rest and feels like a fool. He'll try to do better tonight when she comes over to thank him after her dance. Stevie spots the five as she dips to show him her right breast but doesn't react. Very cool. Sequins fall on either side of the breast. She jiggles, and the left one comes forth as well, sequins now nestled between the two. Carroll looks at the guy next to him; he can't help it, she's sort of in the middle. The guy now has a five out, too.

By her third song (he was right: she's been watching Jasmine) the sequin costume is reduced to a belt of sorts. By the whispers and nudges around the room Carroll can sense that her cleanly shaven crotch has already developed something of a reputation, and he is gladdened by the reverential treatment it seems to be receiving from the men. No stupid remarks. And he'll be damned if she didn't give him an extra second, a private second real close to his face. Probably saw the money, not so much his but the way he started the trend, the proliferation of padded tips along the rail. Probably thinks of him as something of an ally now, and he is of course in a way, inasmuch as they're both concerned with . . . well, Goodness. He watches carefully as she makes her way, man to man, around the stage. There's no way that she spends any extra time with the others, no way. By the time she finishes the set he is certain that she spent at least two or three seconds more in front of him than in front of any of the other men. Even the ones with bigger tips out are probably wondering if they know each other, Carroll and Stevie, wondering if maybe they aren't friends or something. But friends, think about friends. Friends would be nice, or something.

The DJ/doorman starts rambling about whoever is dancing next. But Carroll's not listening; he's getting wound up, tight, twisted, and jumpy with thoughts of their imminent encounter. First she'll come around the stage, holding a light robe loosely around herself and collecting the tips. She'll smile and inaudibly thank the men who have left out a single or two for her. Then—and this is what will be new for Carroll, and it's what has him dry of mouth and wet of palm—she'll retreat to the dressing area, don a slightly more substantial costume appropriate for the floor, and come around to personally thank the three or four men who have left tips of larger denomination. He looks about. Tina is sneaking up on some guy who is always sitting at the bar. This guy likes to lean back on his stool, and she is planning to grab him as if to pull him over all the way. Not a new trick exactly, they both love doing this, and Carroll can't wait for the inevitable fall that will break Tina, the guy, or both of this habit. She's winking at the barmaid. There she goes. The guy yelps and waves his arms in a desperate attempt to regain his balance, like this is a new one on him. What a dope. Tina catches him, the back of his neck against her chest, and this must be the rub, this must be good for a few friendly dollars at some point in the evening. Here comes Stevie inside the rail with just a smile for him as she takes his five. Good. She would have thanked him now if she wasn't planning to return later. Her robe falls open as she squats for a bill, and he realizes that she has no tan lines, nor is she tan, nor is she pale. A lot of the other dancers have tan lines on bottom but none on top. Easy clues, but to what?

After finishing up with her collecting, she disappears behind the curtain again. He is by now well aware of her tendency to take refuge back there, and she'll no doubt take her time changing. No matter. Sooner or later she'll have to talk to him. He's sure of it. He can wait. He can sit here and wait, watch—who is that . . . the new redhead— he can sit here and watch the new redhead and wait.

Like most of the girls who start here, this girl is not without experience. This is clearly evident as soon as she takes the stage. Red hair flying, she becomes practically airborne as she lunges from the curtain to the chain-suspended steel ring that hangs from the ceiling. Eschewed by most of the dancers, this apparatus, when used properly, creates something of a stunning seraphic effect for the men seated at the stage. Redhead swings wide, over her flock. Breasts jut forth in response to centrifugal force, and she makes these rotations as if she owned the air. A knee is bent, other leg straight. Lest her audience grow too comfortable with the vision, she winds down too soon, wrapping to a small fast spin at center stage reminiscent of a skater. This redhead (remember to listen for the name) wears a costume of tight black panties and a chest full of tiny white, pearl-like beads. Sounds silly, but it works. Indeed, those beads know when and where to part, and the men at the stage are, Carroll can see, quick and true fans. Carroll guesses that Redhead is used to such a response; he can see it in her smile, the way she drinks up their adoration, takes to it like a vampire to blood. Old movies on late-night television. Peter Cushing. Christopher Lee. A hundred other guys who never even achieved that modicum of success. So many lost souls before and around him. This girl must have a name, certainly she is an attention grabber. Carroll, of course, is lending only a mild interest—his mind is strictly on Stevie—a sporting interest. It concerns him to see how easily the other men are taken in, and he has to admit that if it weren't for Stevie this redhead would look pretty damn good to him as well. She walks out on her first song before its over, leaving her lovers breathless, confused, and wanting nothing but her return. Carroll raises an eyebrow at this, what he considers an infraction, a breech of agreement, and he wonders how it'll go over with the powers that be. And he wonders when Stevie will come around. And he wonders what the redhead's name is (listen for the DJ/doorman). Wonders what she'll do for the second of three (watch).

And come they do, the words of the DJ/doorman. Come they do, and if history is any guide they probably include the name of this new redhead, pronounced clearly over the room, preceded by not too many desultory remarks, bumps o' the mike, and all-around general static and lack of squelching. Carroll wouldn't know. He would, but his attention is suddenly sucked through the reverse vacuum of his eyes the moment they fall upon Stevie, dressed for the floor and tending to her thank-yous in a fashion more timely than he predicted. She is wearing a white wraparound lace thing, a half robe, and though her breasts are certainly present the effect is surprisingly chaste, and they should present no problem in conversation . . . her breasts. She begins at the far side of the stage. By now the new redhead is dancing her second of three, moving back and forth far too often and using every opportunity to block his line of sight as he watches Stevie thank the big tippers. He is unable to keep tabs on how and how long she is with each man, and he takes solace in the fact that she is saving him for last. More redhead . . . there . . . what? She's been with that guy. . . . He thought— he assumed—that she moved along, but she's still talking to Bachelor Number Two. Way too long, at least twice as long as she spent with the first guy. Now she's laughing. They're both laughing. More redhead. Oh great. She's indicating the booths, showing the guy where to wait for a table dance. What a lowlife, taking advantage of every- body's thank-you time to ask for a table dance. Carroll has half a mind to speak to the manager, but that'll never hap- pen. But again, who knows? He just hopes for Bachelor Number Two's sake that she finishes her thank-yous be- fore skipping over to the booth with him. No. Okay. Well at least he's going alone to wait at the little counter in front of the booths. At least that's something. She wouldn't for- get Carroll. Of course not. It won't be any great joy watch- ing her dance for this guy, and he'd rather not have the additional pressure of thinking about that just when he's trying so hard to keep up the nerve for his thank-you. . . . Okay. No time to worry about it now. One more guy to thank, then Carroll. Here she comes—that was quick, hopes his goes longer—here she comes.

Stevie approaches him. There can be no doubt, for she is looking toward him as if to a destination. His heart is pounding, and by now that is old news. The fact that he's already been through a table dance with this woman, had her topless, inches away from his face, talking to him, does nothing to assuage his perennial anxiety. Reaching his side, she stops, or halts, like it was given to her as a stage direction.

"Thank you," she says, and she offhandedly puts her hand on his back, big-sister-like and in lieu of a peck on the cheek.

But Carroll doesn't see it that way. To him it is suddenly the most affectionate gesture he can imagine. Behind his flushed face and eyes so stinging that he must continually blink at her, he thinks that she's so right, that even this small action is the most brilliantly appropriate thing she could have done. He wants to look around and get the reactions of the men in the room, but he dare not look away from her magnetic half-smile.

". . . welcome," he gets out.

After giving him a little pat to indicate goodbye, she pulls her hand away from his back. He senses this, and realizes that if he has anything to say to her he'd better say it now.

"Table dance . . . remember me?" Though he knows she remembers him from their table dance last night, his mind is a blank, and this is the best he can do on such short notice. He should have had it worked out better, about the clothes. What kind of clothes does she like. And what else? There was something else. He can hardly expect her to do all the talking.

"You want a table dance?" she asks, misunderstanding and with both hands now clasped impatiently in front of her.

He wasn't ready for this, and he's sure he's not ready for another table dance; it's too hard, too much, too much at this point anyway. "No. . . . I had one last night. Do you remember? We talked?" He can feel his shoulders shaking, and he hopes to God she doesn't notice. Should have padded shoulders, like a suit. Little shock absorbers for his nerves.

She sorta remembers. Yeah, she guesses she remembers. "Sure, sure, I remember. We talked, right? Thanks, thanks a lot." Still not sure what he's after, she adds, "Did you want another then? Tonight? I've got a customer waiting, but you can be next if you'd like." She doubts that the guy on deck will go much longer than two dances. She's got time for this guy, and it wouldn't hurt to make up a little work after missing so much of her shift. Yeah, sure, she remembers this guy. He's okay.

Now he's worried that he blew it, led her on, and he wonders if he shouldn't take the dance, if he isn't committed to it. Then he remembers the money. At twenty bucks a song even one would clean him out. He'd have to leave, go home, or go to the ATM and come back, and that would look stupid not to mention cost him another cover charge. He should change the subject, and again he wishes he could remember what he wanted to talk to her about; it seems he had something in mind.

"Well maybe later, or tomorrow. I mean I want one, but I can't right now . . . so maybe later." Now he's sure she can see him shaking. "Shirts," he says, real sudden. "Do you like curlicues? On shirts, I mean. Do you like curlicues on shirts? Do you like shirts with curlicues on them?" Caught up in the question, the proper phrasing of it, he's almost dancing around in his seat, delivering the lines in verse.

Yeah, now she remembers this guy. He's gotta be harmless, even cute. So many puppies looking for a teat to suck on. "Sure, I like shirts with curlicues. Do you?" Funny, how now she's got him placed it's so easy to respond to this stupid question. Sweet, really. He's sweet in his way.

Now he's just rolling. He's a ball, and he's just rolling. And it's easy, it's too good, like a gutter ball in bowling, no effort. "Oh yes! I like them just fine. I have some (a small lie: he will have some). I'll wear it. . . . I mean I'll wear them here."

She's busting. Oh, what a sweet little ninny he is! Can't laugh in his face though, not this one. "Do," she says, smiling widely as a compromise to her insistent laughter. "Do," she repeats, all she can get out. She's gonna lose it, so quick as a tick she tags his cheek with a kiss and then leaps off, away. She walks away. Sweet, really. Curlicues, oh God!

It's like a movie. He can just see things happening around him. This may be the happiest moment of his life. He's always wanted to make this statement, but now that he has he realizes how limiting it is, depressing almost. No matter, he was right! He thought she liked him, and he was right. A kiss. Right here in front of the world, she kissed him. He should know by now: there are good days and bad days, but they're always mixed up in the same day. Stevie's there, Solo's there (somewhere), things are in place. He sits down, all grin, watches the new redhead without really seeing her. Third of three. Gotta get her name.

But he can't help but notice, maybe more now because of the shirt than anything else, that Redhead is spending a fair amount of time with Curlicue. She's kneeling before him from the stage with her face much too close to his, close like should only be in a table dance. He's got one of those smug right-where-I-want-her grins, the son of a bitch. Must be that damn shirt. Now she's leaning over him, squatted sort of, ass up in the air, tits in his face, and all that long red hair covering swinging around his head, tickling the back of his neck, covering him like a little tent. There's only two lousy bucks in front of the guy, so what gives with the special treatment? Maybe he's her boyfriend. They're not supposed to be in here, the boyfriends, but Carroll's seen stuff like this before, especially with new girls, whose boyfriends can get in with the crowd because they're not yet recognized by the management. It never seems to last though; somehow they always find out. As a test Carroll puts two bills out on the rail, even timing it so that she happens to look around right as they go up. Sure enough she wraps up Curlicue in short order and swings over to Carroll, almost as if she'd been waiting the whole time for him to finish up that other business and start flashing some green. He thinks maybe the girl is just hungry, maybe just liking her new job, digging the new gig, Chase would say. She does seem to be enjoying herself, and while he doesn't get the full hair-breast treatment, he does get more than he's used to getting.

Salaciously she licks her lips for him, like a *Penthouse* magazine photo, only moving. "Is this your little bell?" she wants to know, reaching for something at his shoulder. "Is this how I call you?"

Carroll can't figure out what the heck she's talking about and has to pull himself away from her so-close lips in order to check out his shoulder and hopefully offer a response. She's tugging a piece of his shirt. This stupid shirt that his aunt sent him has those stupid buttoned shoulder things like on a uniform that you're supposed to keep gloves or a hat or something under. Epaulets. He always assumed they were phony and didn't even unbutton, but fuck if one didn't unbutton itself, the goofy strap hanging sloppily off his shoulder, a nerd ID badge, like a pocket protector or a sign that says KICK ME. He almost fumbles and tries to rebutton it, but pulls his hand back in time when he realizes that that would necessitate brushing her off, her playful fingers.

"I guess it came unbuttoned," he says stupidly. And worse: "I hate this shirt, my aunt sent it to me." Great. He feels himself blush and wonders why it took so long. Seen too many tits, maybe, breasts.

She smiles, still flirting, and he can see that she's willing to tolerate him. Two bucks is two bucks. "Well we'll just have to get you a new shirt," she suggests, rising and preparing to make center stage for the end of the song.

So it was Curlicue's shirt that caught her attention! Amazing. Amazing yet the coincidence. Unable to resist the opportunity for a second opinion, he asks her, "You like curlicues?" though he feels the answer is obvious.

She cocks her head, still flirty enough to make it seem like she's secretly pleased by the unexpected query. "You like curlicues?" she asks, or says, or repeats. He can't tell, she's turned her back and gone her saucy way.

Saturdaysunday

Saturday morning bright and early he walks down to the corner for a cup of coffee and a paper. Normally he would drive, being uncomfortable walking in his heart-of-Hollywood neighborhood, but most of the more threatening inhabitants of Hollywood Boulevard are not around in the morning. They're sleeping, temporarily cloistered in their gritty holes in the wall, abject and miserable, he imagines, in their inchoate contrition, unsure of why they feel bad about the horrors of the night before and waiting like a time bomb to explode and lash out at their detestable accomplices. Such is the life of the bad guy on television, and Carroll feels comfortable with this portrait. Coffee, too, is not part of his usual routine. Think about all those ads on TV for decaffeinated coffee, hardly any for regular. There must be something wrong with the stuff, something they're not telling us . . . yet. Wean us off with the placebo before it's too late. Congressmen's daughters must be getting sick, a quiet panic. He's always eschewed anything he notices other people craving. Guys at work, always the coffee in one fist to balance out the law book in the other, torn pieces of paper page markers sticking out sloppily like so many tentacles. Still, he feels randy, and one cup might be fun. It's not like he's never tasted the stuff. Best to drink it now and then so you can be part of the class-action suit that's inevitably coming.

The paper is a thorn in his side. He hates to buy it. Hates to spend the money when the deadbeat across the hall—well down the hall actually but it still rankles—gets the damn thing delivered every day only to let them sit outside his door and pile up for weeks on end until the maintenance man has to haul them away in that enormous plastic wheelbarrow the size of a Dumpster and just as smelly, lets them sit and rot, turn yellow despite the dark-ness in the hallway. Oh! but God forbid anyone should touch one of those papers, anyone like Carroll, who after taking out the trash one day returned to his own floor and happened to notice a story on the front page of one of the papers—unclear even if it was that day's edition—that caught his attention, and rather than up and take the dis-carded piece of trash as would be his obvious right and no court in the land would argue, he stood there like a dope, reading it in the hall, or starting to read it but not getting far before Deadbeat yanks open his door (Carroll had never seen the guy before and he looked bad, dirty and pathetic like one of those TV bad guys) and says, "Can I help you?" shouting it real mean and making it sound more like *What the fuck are you doing outside of my door?* "No," Carroll muttered. "Sorry." Scampered back to his own apartment, where he remained all day wishing he had that paper so he could look for a new place to live though that thought eventually went the way of the maintenance man's next wheelbarrow load, and indeed, months later when he found himself cornered in the elevator with Deadbeat the guy acted like he'd never before laid eyes on Carroll, who, of course, endured the ride somewhat less comfortably.

What he is seeking this morning in his bold foray into the universal clique of Styrofoam coffee cups and segmented newspapers is information on where to go for some new clothes, threads, Chase would say. Ads, subliminally lodged behind his eyes from being flashed before him on television, for department stores and their sales, should, he hopes, have less glitzy but more informative siblings hidden somewhere in the folds of Saturday's *Los Angeles Times*. The Broadway, Bullock's, the May Company, Nordstrom, names that he knows he's seen, places that must sell clothing, nice clothing, but he needs a hotter trail. The ads, the TV ads, always turn him off for some reason. Odd, then, how he remembers so well the even cheesier ads for 976 chat lines and pitches for party-line phone sex delivered by lascivious-looking (but always flawed) women holding princess phones and pining for verbal company. Who could have predicted this industry? They knew about computers, they knew about cocaine, they probably even knew about music video, but who ever would have guessed that phone sex would become the burgeoning industry it seems to be. Response to AIDS, he considers, and immediately feels out of his depth, like this is stuff best left to the commentators who follow the local news, purporting to be station manager or maybe news director. Those guys use words like AIDS as if they're supposed to, get away with saying stuff that would embarrass Carroll to death if he ever tried it. Condom. Lesbian. Words best left in print. After all, what does he know about sex? This is the place: GYROS, FALAFEL, HAMBURGERS, TACOS, OPEN 7:00AM, and underneath it all a hand-drawn cup of coffee with three squiggly lines rising out of it to indicate how hot it really is. This place, he's seen it before, it'll do fine. It even has a little wraparound counter and some refolded newspapers strewn about the stool tops. A guy in an apron-protected silk shirt collects shavings from a sweating column of unidentifiable meat, makes a sandwich, and hands it to a customer with already greasy lips. At this hour! Glazed and powdered donuts sit atop the counter. Carroll's speed.

Two glazed and one powdered, exactly, a small black on the side, as ordered, augmented at the last moment with Moca-Mix from a warm commercial carton, as consumed, just like at Winchell's when he stopped to use the bathroom . . . had to be four, five months ago. The Moca–Mix carton is sitting in a stainless-steel pan full of water-once-ice, which Carroll knocks as he reaches for it, causing it to splash around. This elicits a suspicious look from the mustard-colored chef, who decides that it might be a good time to renew the ice and mitigate future spilling. To him Carroll looks like someone who is destined to add more cream to his coffee as soon as room is made in the Styrofoam cup. To Carroll the chef looks displeased at this unforeseen chore, and he guesses that he's now persona non grata at this place. He decides to lie low, burying himself in the paper and propitiously coming up with a full-page ad for the Semi-Annual Men's Sale at the Broadway. Locations are listed, and it is decided that the Beverly Center—though the garage parking confused and intimidated him when he was there last year, causing him to lose his ticket and pay without argument a full day's rate for what should have been three hours free—is the place to go. Hastily he finishes his breakfast, avoiding the eyes of Mustard Chef and leaving a quarter on the counter as a compromise between leaving nothing and leaving a real tip. He can never tell at a place like this. Sometimes they have little baskets that say *Thank You!* and this is nice because you know what to do, and because the clinking of coins sounds the same even if you don't put in a lot.

Thus energized, if not excessively nourished, he takes to the star-studded sidewalk for the jaunt back to his apartment. It's getting warm. Busses everywhere blow huge brown clouds of particulate exhaust, so heavy they visibly hold their space like small patches of fog. Hollywood Boulevard, both ways, vanishes into these clouds; they hold the secrets of the vanishing point. Men and women asleep on the sidewalk are covered in a layer of real soot on the outside and no doubt on the inside as well. Tourists just hitting town from the heartland try hard not to look too discouraged at their first glimpse of the glamour. Those heading out to the airport peer around hopefully for the basis of a found memory. These people—here comes a family now, Mom and Dad in matching *I Survived a Tour of the Stars' HORMONES* tees, Son and Daughter looking despondent, cause unclear—worry Carroll. He knows they're going home unhappy, embarrassed to have shared in this vacation error and ashamed to talk it out among themselves. Though they wonder if maybe things turned out this way through some deficiency within themselves, like someone who can't scare up a conversation at a party, still they have unanimously taken private vows never to return here. It's on their faces and may come out tangentially in an argument over finances next month. Then the floodgates will open, and Carroll will almost be able to hear the shouting from Ohio. Ohio. What must such a place be like? Why would they leave only to willingly hasten home. Carroll's never traveled on a vacation, never left the area around Los Angeles.

At home, still thinking of soot, he washes his face and then heads down to his Vega. Soot everywhere in the garage, both brought in and generated here, or is it just busses? The car starts right up, no problem, and once out of the garage he turns onto Hawthorne to the corner and Orange. That to Sunset, to La Cienega, that part where the hill is so steep that he hates to come the other way and have to work the clutch so fast, it slipping bad enough as it is anyway and the hill not helping matters. But down is okay, and La Cienega goes right past the Beverly Center. There's an entrance to the tricky garage on that side, no problem.

The garage is under the mall but above ground. So the first through the fifth floor (level?) is all garage, and then there are three levels of shopping. Carroll forgets this and, after changing his mind about his parking spot twice and ending up at last on the fourth level near the Beverly Boulevard escalator, travels down to street level via two moving staircases and walks precipitously down a third that is broken and inexplicably tougher to negotiate than a real staircase, which after all doesn't move anyway, before catching up with his error and finding himself on the street with a group of tourists waiting to get in to the Hard Rock Cafe. A great pall of airborne grease hangs outside this place, and though it turns Carroll's stomach the tourists seem not to mind standing in it like it's some great gaseous preview trailer for the restaurant, or some odoriferous hors d'oeuvre for which they will later be charged along with the City of Angels Sacred Cowburgers: *No mistake, sir, that's the Fat o'Gristle Smog Inhalant Plate, which you and your family enjoyed on our patio prior to being seated.* This cloud must always be here; Carroll remembers it from the last time he found himself standing in front of the Hard Rock Cafe, the last time he made this same mistake with the escalators, the last and only other time he was ever at the Beverly Center. He endures the by now endless ride back up. All the up escalators work fine, no surprise there, and he arrives at last on level six, the first shopping level, being dumped off the top of the escalator like a bale of hay in a loft.

Bullock's department store is the first thing he sees, BULLOCK'S, if the sign is to be believed. So he was wrong about the Beverly Boulevard escalator and will have to walk to the other end of the mall to find the Broadway, right next to the La Cienega Boulevard escalator, he remembers from last time. Should have left the car in that first parking space. No big deal, he'll walk across the mall and maybe even find some shirts along the way, though it won't be the Semi-Annual Men's Sale anywhere but the Broadway. But there are sales. Right away he hits a men's store with a big hand-lettered banner in the window that proclaims UP TO 70% OFF—AND MORE! The store is called Casa Nova, and the only people in it are two well-oiled and suited, mustached salesmen looking out at him with their hands folded behind their backs. Carroll's not sure he wants to be in the store alone with these guys, and, as if sensing his trepidation, one of the men shrugs and bends down, picks up a bottle of Windex and a roll of paper towels, and returns to wiping the front of a glass case. Just then two large women, shopping-bag mountains in motion, push past him into the store and take up with the other salesman. Carroll follows, and Windex is on him in no time.

"Hello," he intones, taking in at a glance Carroll's tricolored polo and brown polyester slacks. With meaning: "Just let me know if there's anything that I can do for you."

Carroll, feeling captured and released under surveillance, nods: okay, yeah, and commences what he expects to be a brief look around the place. But there are many things to see, and he has been out of the loop, to put it gently. Silk shirts in bright colors and intricate patterns abound, slashed, so slashed, slashed so that the prices are too low even to divulge on the tags. Rather a calculation is required, involving the red-pen price under the crossed-out marked price and application of the formula *ALL Shirts an Additional 20% OFF Ticketed Prices* and, in Carroll's case, at least at this early stage, further adjustment to the tune of *Cash Buyers Receive 5% OFF on ALL Purchases.* In most cases these formulae bring the final price of a crossed-out $145 shirt down to $24, but even this is undermined at the last moment by Windex, who upon noticing any customer pausing at or near any piece of merchandise, materializes at the side of said customer and confides in a conspiratorial tone something like, in this case, "Twenty bucks."

"Really?" says Carroll, tugging on the sleeve of a blue jobbie with, yes, gold curlicues. That's a table dance, he reminds himself. "Only twenty bucks?"

This is so good that Windex practically throws down his paper towels. "Yes, sir. These are going fast . . . in fact . . . (inspecting the tag). Hey Rudy! These Palomas aren't supposed to be on sale, are they?"

"Palomas? No, I don't think so," recites Rudy from the register.

A concerned look visits Windex's face. Carroll waits, feeling queasy about causing this kind of trouble and hoping he's not committed to paying a hundred and forty-five bucks for this shirt that he had merely touched in passing.

"Well it's marked down here, and I just told this customer that I'd sell it for twenty bucks," argues Windex.

"Then I guess you're gonna have to sell it for twenty bucks, but the boss is gonna kill you. . . . Oh, what the heck: do twenty, we could use the numbers." Rudy returns to his register; this then is the final judgment.

Use the numbers, thinks Carroll.

"You heard him," admits Windex.

"Why don't you try it on, sir," suggests Rudy, now through with his ladies and unable to hold his tongue. He loves this stuff, maybe too much.

"M," reads Windex, checking the size and removing the shirt from the hanger. "Oh yeah, this'll fit you just fine, especially at twenty bucks, huh?" He chuckles and winks at Carroll. Now it's the three of them against the boss, who must be at lunch, or off today.

"That's okay," says Carroll, loathing the idea of undressing and dressing in one of the little plywood closets in the rear of the store, doors so badly fitted that anyone would be able to see through the cracks. "M is my size, I'll buy it." He smiles weakly, feels kinda strange. "Oh," he dares, fishing frantically in his pocket for the evidence. "I have cash. I'll pay for it with cash. Is that an extra five percent off?"

"What—Hey Rudy! He wants five percent for cash!— what? Are you trying to kill me?"

Out. Finally. Something wrong with that guy, but an okay shirt, and that does it, he's going straight to the Broadway. Someplace reputable. Big.

But before he can make it to that end of the mall he sees this girl (sort of cute but no Stevie), salesgirl, must be . . . yeah, salesgirl, smiling at him from behind the glass of a shop called Eclecticution. The place is dark and the crowd is young, but this girl looks friendly enough and he goes in and she just *loves* curlicues and thinks they would look great on him but maybe he should consider some other prints as well like say . . . oh maybe . . . this piece here with the little dragons on the sleeves and the big one on the back and he really doesn't think so, well how about, well then that's fine, how about this one with these so very fine fine green and aqua lines that blend into swirls, which are really like curlicues anyway and don't they look great with your eyes and the shirt is on him and her hands are on him and it really doesn't look half bad those fine lines and what the heck he takes it and the socks

well I don't know okay now how about some jeans
and you'll be all set and jeans yikes watch out for those
hands and even on sale that's two table dances. Well now,
baby, I kinda dig the way you're flashin' those threads.
Hands like a pussy. Clothes like condoms. Oh fuck! I'll buy
anything!

More bags, more shops. The MasterCard that he
keeps strictly for emergencies (and the bimonthly dinner
out just so the bank knows he hasn't died) is crying for
mercy. Carroll has begun to use phrases like: *You take credit
cards, right?* and *Could I put this on my MasterCard?*, and even
found himself avoiding one store on which the little credit
card decal was conspicuously absent. Which decal—
indeed, in this case a sculpted brass icon—he spots with
some relief from a distance on the marble facade that surrounds the prodigious entrance to the Broadway, which
he has, at last, reached. There he goes. Right away they
sell him two large and handled shopping bags for a quarter apiece from a sort of honor-system vending machine.
The barges of shopping, and he loads all his other bags
into them and heads for Men's.

And wouldn't you know it! The Broadway doesn't
have a single thing that suits him, and isn't it lucky that
he had the foresight to make those other stops. He buys a
package of underwear to obviate any guilt he might feel
in getting the parking validation that he declined at each
and every one of the other stores, thinking that the big
spending would happen here. This done, he heads back
to the Vega, finds it after only two wrong levels (floors?).

Head for home. Solid afternoon now, but an anticipated late night at Indiscretions will give him time to re-
view his purchases. Radio. Rap music. Okay, why not. One

look at the bags in the seat next to him reminds Carroll that all bets are off. This is a new age. For that matter every age must be a new age. Solo is missing, Stevie is here. No shoes, and that wasn't easy after the virtual foot massage from the rather effeminate clerk, moussed and labeled *Chaz*. Name tag gleamed with reflected fluorescents, and Carroll had to admit that the attention really wasn't half bad, and that there are worlds of activity out there that he'll never come close to knowing, and that how bad can it be when anybody likes anybody else, no matter why or what the reason for. Traffic has that nasty amateur rush-hour quality of Saturday afternoons. Weekdays, at least, carry rules of misconduct. The rap follows too closely the traffic, and for that reason it bugs him and he turns it off. The general flow of things up La Cienega causes him to miss the Santa Monica Boulevard turn, and he gets rail-roaded into making that clutch-slipping climb up to Sunset that he hates. But it goes okay, and he supposes that this time he knew it would.

Billboards loom large here on this stretch of Sunset, many of them private insider stuff: *Film San Antonio* or *Academy Members—For Your Consideration. . . .* Expensive hotels, private clubs, restaurants he would never have the nerve to walk into, just driving on the street here makes him feel like he crashed a party and the bouncer is looking for him to kick his ass out of here. Past the intersection at Crescent Heights though it gets better, grittier, and while he doesn't feel any more at home here, he can count on the fact that no one would notice or care. There's a burger place on the right, and he catches sight of, peeking out from the back of the white brick structure, a streetwalker, is a good name for this girl, a hooker. A long-time Hollywood

resident, Carroll knows one of these girls when he sees
her, and seeing one of these girls is something that rarely
happens anymore. Not so long ago they lined Sunset from
here to past Western like so many hymnals down the back
of a church pew. Now gone. Swept away. He wonders what
they could have done to incur such genocide, wonders what
he could have done to overcome his confounded fear and
muster the nerve to engage one of them, or at the very least
to offer some verbal declination in response to their intrigu-
ing solicitations, accosting him at red lights. Once one
tapped on his passenger window and with a heaving
motion brought forth from her sweater a bosom that
was really too small to bring off the trick, though this girl
acted unaware, handled herself as if she were a legend
of the streets. He simply drove away, looking straight
ahead, eyeing her in his rearview mirror, a wound on his
windshield.

Coming back this way he likes to make the left at La
Brea and up to Hawthorne from there, provided that the
left-turn bay isn't too full. If it is he can always cruise on by
to Orange, a contingency plan that in the past has bought
him horns from behind as he struggles to position himself for the unpainted left there, just a yellow diagonal
slash due to the fact that the intersection jogs and they
probably don't know what else to paint there. The garage,
when he finally reaches it after almost being assaulted by
a gang of black boys jaywalking on Hawthorne and giving
him looks so nasty that he wished he had left the rap music
on the radio but didn't really think that that would've
helped matters just the same, is choked with exhaust fumes.
Last year the ventilation fans broke down, and no one was
allowed to get to their cars all morning; maybe this is the

same problem, maybe he's the first to discover it and should report it. But no, the maintenance man is there in the corner, fooling around with a large pipe, which doesn't quite look like it would be part of the ventilation—water is leaking from the pipe—but surely the guy must realize that he can hardly breathe. For Carroll's part, his eyes are watering and he feels lightheaded. He can only hope that Maintenance doesn't decide to take a nap behind the Dumpster, but there's no way he's gonna bother that guy again, not after the light incident.

Gathering his parcels, he hurries to the elevator, which is not quite as bad as the garage, and makes it nonstop to his floor. Safely in his apartment, first thing, he turns on the television, just for some company. He gets it in the form of . . . they look like chimpanzees. Yes, four of them, four of them in a row, separated by plywood partitions, each one half-heartedly, in that distracted way that chimps have, manipulating a joystick-like control that is mounted on a panel on their laps. This evidently being done in response to some off-camera stimulus in front of them, the plywood perhaps to keep them from seeing the responses of their fellows, keep them from cheating, or maybe they just like their privacy. It all looks pretty familiar to Carroll, who figures that these chimps are unlikely to do anything different today than they did yesterday, or whenever they were last subjected to this. Face it: even if one of them did something prodigious, say managed to design and construct a new microchip, an ozone patch, or a reusable spacecraft, we'd never take it seriously. Too close to home, too scary, too many potentially disorganized religions. Now a researcher, a not unattractive woman in a white lab coat (but still the legs sticking out), approaches chimp number two. She is explaining something that neither Carroll nor the chimp wants to listen to; it will only complicate their lives. But the chimp seems to dig it when she touches his head. Probably to him she is God, and Carroll has to admit that he kind of likes this woman too. She's got things covered.

Well enough of this. Though he's growing weary of the whole concept—not to mention guilty over the expense—it's time to try on clothes. Not as free as the dancing he did earlier in the week, trying on new clothes, alone with only a mirror, seems very narcissistic, a tribute to himself not the dancers, very commercial, like giving up, like when he tries something small, say this pair of socks, adds the shirt just like the girl told him to, something this small and it still pains him to waltz in front of the mirror. It pains him so much that he does it twice, then again. And again, same socks, same shirt, now a little music to cover the noise of the television. He hates looking at himself, but when he invades the mirror for the fifth time in the same clothes he knows, like picking a scab, that he'll do it again. This mirror is filthy. It's cracked in the corner where it got screwed in too tightly. Always been dirty and always been cracked, long as Carroll can remember, from the first day he moved in, and that was a long time ago. He doesn't like the place any better now than when he was scrubbing that first night and trying to convince himself he hadn't made a mistake. Been here forever and won't ever leave. Reminds him of Melissa at Indiscretions. She's none too happy, no secret there. Always the same dance for that girl, been there forever but can't walk off the stage. She hates those men for liking her, but that only makes them like her more. Carroll wonders what it would be like to sit down and talk with her, talk right past those big breasts. What then? Does she quit? Does he move?

Time for another bag. Whaddawehavehere. . . ? Jeans. Green jeans, as a matter of fact, like Mr. Greenjeans on the old *Captain Kangaroo*. But these are green Guess jeans, probably outside the poor farmer's budget. Was he the one with the bunny puppet? Was he the reason Carroll bought green jeans today? The reason Guess makes them? Sinister, that old guy, like the decaf coffee thing. They look okay, but what? is he supposed to wear them only with these socks and shirt? Then it looks too well planned, or maybe not; he wishes he knew more about this stuff, might've been better to have a salesgirl who was less pretty and more honest. Maybe she was, how would he know? Hit the mirror. And again. Okay. Enough of that one. Once more, then off. He grabs another bag, the first one. What was it? Oh yeah, blue with gold curlicues. Let's see—oh man, he looks scrawny. Get that thing buttoned!

Well, maybe . . . but he doubts that it should be worn with these green jeans. Just a hunch, but it does seem awfully colorful. He goes to another bag, soon another yet. The many combinations take hold, chuck the bags, empty, crumpled bags, about the room. Spent vessels. Carroll waxes the reluctant model, an end-of-summer twelve-year-old being cajoled by a weary school-spent mom into each of his new fall outfits. Parade around the kitchen for your father. But Carroll is alone, and he finds that the longer this self-imposed torture drags on, the longer he spends on each visit in front of the mirror. Some sort of silent revenge, like maybe if he works hard enough he can wear out the mirror, wear out all mirrors and never have to look at himself again.

He bought so much stuff that none of it feels like his, like the only way to have so many new things around is to be at someone else's house. Tags are saved along with the receipts in one of the smaller bags set aside for this purpose. Less fortunate bags are uncrumpled, folded, and stacked. Wayward threads are carefully clipped from new garments, an anxious twinge snapping his gut at each snip. Wet towels in the locker room and somebody's gonna get hurt. By evening he's reached and gone beyond his saturation point. He never did have much of an eye for this stuff, and now each outfit is merely a minor variation on The Same. He's got to make a decision on what to wear tonight. It's Saturday and the club will steam along hard into the wee hours, so he can push it a little, not be there so early. But on the other hand it's Saturday, and he doesn't want to miss anything. Night of hopeful significance, it's bred into our genes. Wonder if it's a special night in jails? That would be easy, wear only black and white stripes— but then that's gotta be strictly movie stuff. Naked and bemused, he postpones his decision and climbs into the shower for some distance, and to be that much closer to ready.

It works. Emerging from the shower—wade the little lake that he can't believe isn't caused by the crack on the bottom of the frosted plastic door, though the maintenance man says it's only a hairline and that all the stalls have them—he is decided. He is committed to wearing a black shirt with blacker curlicues raised all over it, a shirt he didn't remember buying until he opened the bag. The shirt then as a given, he'll wear whatever pants fall into line— he supposes the green jeans will do—and with this resolution in place he towels himself, a bit more cheerily than he might have otherwise. Braced up, he is, for the evening, and he sets about the preparations, later the dressing.

By the time he heads down to the Vega it's past eight. Traffic flow no problem, as if in accordance with an unspoken citywide agreement to not mess up anybody's Saturday night plans. At the club the lot is packed, and he's stuck with the alley. But he doesn't give it another thought, so focused is he on seeing Stevie tonight. When he stepped in front of the mirror for the final time tonight he knew that he looked about as presentable as he will ever look, and thus the last obstacle had been removed. Tonight he will talk with her. If necessary he'll buy a table dance. He's got money, he made sure, over a hundred dollars, enough over that he could buy five table dances if he had to and still have enough for drinks and cover and dollar tips. He locks the Vega, doesn't look back (well, maybe once, just to make sure that he didn't leave the lights on), and crunches across the gravel to the front of the club.

". . . name of Tasha, gentlemen, put your hands together for the lovely Tasha. Tasha will be right back for the third of three . . . no . . . yes, the third of three, gentlemen. Remember that Tasha, and all our lovelyladies, are available for those private topless table dances. Just ask—"

A scratch and squeal rip through the speakers, cutting off the DJ/doorman and quitting as abruptly as they began. Carroll moves to the admission booth, pays his cover, and passes through the curtain. Tasha. He recalls a Tasha here about six months ago, but she left; left, he always suspected, under suspicious circumstances. He knows no details, but the last night he saw her here was coincidentally the same night as one of the few skirmishes in the history of Indiscretions, that is to say the portion of that history which includes Carroll as a witness. Not much to report, really. Just a guy rising from a booth in the middle of his table dance and calling for the manager, Carroll watching from across the room. Tasha, a disgusted look on her face, sauntered off to the ladies' room, never came out? Maybe? In any case that was the last that Carroll ever saw of her at the club. Manager calmed customer, who left anyway. Details were not forthcoming, and if they were Carroll wouldn't have known where to listen. If such a thing happened today, he supposes, he could ask Stevie about it. Such are the benefits of being well connected.

The club is crowded. Tight air holds shredded conversation like a dirty vacuum bag, splotchy lumps, that uneasy murmur that lurks between songs here. The DJ/doorman is evidently working to fix that—witness the desultory knocks and hums from the speakers. This girl (lots of new girls lately) this girl Tasha is yet to be revealed, lurking in the dressing area, preparing for her third of three, it was, the DJ/doorman said. There's not much available in the way of seating, and Carroll's ready to settle for a wall space when he sees a chair behind him. On less busy nights this is the on-deck area for the table dances, a place for men to await their favorite lovelylady, or for Man and Favorite Lovelylady to await the timely punctuation of a new song, though Lovelylady, of course, never sits and Man always does, the club perhaps being uncomfortable with a standing man. But on busy nights like tonight the area is given to regular use by regular guys, at the early stage of being merely potential table dance consumers. The whole thing likely sits better with fire code enforcers, having asses in seats, that is, and Carroll quickly takes this chair in the erstwhile on-deck area. After all, there may yet be table dances. There may yet be.

Dchooo dchooo, electronic synth-o-thunder chases smoke about the room. New music on old speakers, naked girl out of curtain. It is the Tasha that he knows from before. Not that she knows him, of course. Nevertheless he has a slight feeling of warmth, insofar as his relations with dressed or undressed women go, a feeling of longtimenoseeness. Silly, but it's nice to know that people aren't dead. Tasha is pretty much the same girl he remembers: five-five, one-fifteen, medium breasts that look a bit pointier than most, especially under the sheer tops that she likes (or used to like) to wear open, shoulder-length sandy blond hair that matches all over, and a pretty face, sharp, with a hard-to-identify English look to it though he doubts she has an accent and in any case has never heard her speak.

As she falls to it Carroll recalls her routine with crystal clarity. Tasha dances with her pussy. Way more than any of the other girls, like in a different league, this being largely a breast place. Oh sure, all the dancers pay lip service, placing their pretty behinds in your face as they bend forward and wink at you from in between their pretty legs. Occasionally a girl will even feign masturbation, her fingers gliding over her pubic hair or wrapped around some imaginary cylinder, but this is sometimes crude and is kept to quick corner gestures, close-in with known customers. Tasha, now Tasha is a different story, and evidently little has changed. He watches her saunter directly to a corner, put one leg up on the brass rail and part wide her thighs for the benefit of the two or three men who are favored with a propitious angle. She puts down her open hands, one on each inner thigh, squeezing her own tender flesh, stretching what she can out of the club rules, inspecting herself right along with her audience, a gynecological flair. Satisfied with the state of things, she looks to the men, studies their faces, as if to say: *Have you seen this? Take a look-see down here.* Snap shut the thighs . . . maybe not quite that quickly. In any event she is off, a moment spent center stage in an obligatory tit twirl-heel down and the stage is her compass—before strolling off to another corner. The guys don't know what to make of her; they hate being second-guessed like this. A bit of a shame, he remembers, in all the time she was dancing here and he was watching, Carroll never saw her up close. He was always seated elsewhere, never at a chosen spot along the rail. Tasha, again, unlike most of the girls, never covers the whole stage during any one song, or set for that matter. She is a very specific girl. Carroll decides he likes her, likes her because she had trouble with management, likes her because, in a way, she makes a joke out of what she's doing, likes her because she's a free agent, free from right and wrong.

Stevie's here, he notices right off, chatting with that new redhead; ought to get her name tonight. Tasha looks to be wrapping up, leaving a side rail where some guy is blinking in confusion; probably saw more than he wanted to. DJ/doorman makes it known that Sylvia will be dancing next, and that we should all be sure to lay a little green on Tasha, whom some of us may remember from olden times at the club and who is now finally back from her extended vacation. DJ/doorman admonishes us fellas not to read too much into said vacation. DJ/doorman remarks that he's sure we'll all agree that it's the same old Tasha. This seat, near the booths and new to Carroll, has its advantages. Like before at the bar, he has a bird's-eye view of things, a step up, this one. Stevie's arrival at the club has done many things on many levels. Profound things on which he dwells constantly, but nice touches as well, like shaking him around this room. For months he would sit in the same place, always careful to arrive early enough to not be shut out, almost growing roots into the crusty carpeting beneath a wobbly chair, random spot on the side of the stage. Circumstances now are otherwise, and he likes not knowing until the last minute where he'll be sitting, sizing up the room like James Bond entering a casino, off-handedly being shaken about the place by Stevie's playful hand, one special bean in a bag.

Here comes Tasha for her take. Tamara, who seems to be working more nights these days, is attentively watching her, he notices, from just outside the ladies' room, ostensibly talking with a customer who is so transfixed by her tits that he doesn't catch her wayward eye, goes right on chatting like he's the fucking center of her world. Wonder if she likes Tasha, or is she a spy for management? Wonder what it's like for two girls in love—same cake with different frosting? Tasha's too much: her set is over and still she's giving them more than they bargained for. Wearing a wraparound skirtlike cloth, she just snatched up a five spot from the rail. Hand carries bill under skirt and comes out empty. Carroll saw it, the guy who put out the five did too, nobody else, not even Tamara. The guy laughs nervously. That was her last tip to collect this set, so Tasha vanishes behind the curtain, that five-dollar bill most likely under a garter.

Sabrina strolls by and smiles at him. He's gotta admit it: he feels pretty sharp in these new clothes. Some gooey love song from the seventies starts up, one of those songs that everyone seemed to like at the time but that today sounds adolescent. Carroll learned to be an adult in the seventies and this is what he came up with. Stuck with it. Sylvia sticks her head out from behind the curtain to get a look at the crowd—like it's changed in the last few minutes since she was out here—and whatever she sees doesn't do much to chase away the doleful look on her face. Discouraged, finally, maybe, Carroll thinks, about having the smallest chest at the club. Still, she gets her share of table dances, and he often wonders if guys don't cotton to her because they think she'll be grateful for the attention . . . and do what for them? Be Real Nice? Sometimes you look at her face and have to grab a fast clue of yourself, real quick and just to recall what's what, like saliva in your mouth, or maybe the way your shoe feels untied. Then you think about what money can't buy. Sylvia's pretty groovy. It can't be very easy for her, yet here she is.

She finally comes out—a little too far into the song so your first impression is to think, Hey! I've been cheated, until you remember that your cover charge bought an endless stream of bare asses, asses past, asses that will come again, asses yet to be scrutinized—and Carroll, though he doesn't even know her, knows right away that she's not herself. First off, not three steps out of the curtain, she stumbles, stumbles, but recovers so languidly that half the men who notice (Sylvia never really rivets the crowd) think it's part of her imperfect dancing. Carroll knows better, and he makes a point of watching her carefully: a concerned father, a worried son, an empathetic sister. Her movements are uneven at best, but her dancing is always like that. It's just that tonight she's uneven in different spots, something he can't point out but knows is there, like a smudge on his sunglasses. You're looking out, something's wrong. Sylvia hits the floor. Not that she falls, no, she drops to her knees, a strictly technical difference in this place. She leans backward, arching her back and exposing her precious-little tits to the glimmer of the mirrored ball. It's a suppliant posture, but her heart's not in it. Her pussy—call it her cunt—is wide open to suggestion. And suggestion is forthcoming in the form of ones and ones, dollars on the rail, more ones. And Sylvia's eyes roll up, not so much unnaturally, but still in that way you don't like to look at. She stays there through the end of the song, this, the first of three. Doesn't even bother to get up, to go backstage and change—why should she, she's already as naked as you get. She *is* naked, first of three and she's already naked. Strange he didn't notice earlier. Should've spotted it the moment she came on stage. Of course the costumes can get pretty skimpy, and it probably doesn't matter all that much, but still he's never seen another girl do it. Cut-to-the-chase Sylvia, we'll call her. She lies there through the break, eyes glassy, slowly blinking. Music starts, second of three. As it picks up so does she, not that anyone looked all that worried. Maybe Carroll.

Who now looks away. These attenuated pokes around the stage are not exactly encouraging fare, and encouragement is exactly what he's looking for. Stevie is a specific activity too, insofar as what he is doing tonight. It's what he was doing all day, his clothes shopping, small offering. Now she's with him, in this room. Again he spots her. His eyes linger as she talks on, unaware of him (or is she), evidently wrapping up her chat with the new redhead. Against his better judgment he holds his gaze. Those things are magnets, gazes, and sure enough she looks up and catches his eye. There they are. He's winging it, terrified to be doing this so boldly (at all), terrified to back away and live forever with that breach of faith, searching her face for a sign of recognition. And she does see him, has seen him enough by now to not be surprised, or even put off by his infatuation. It's not like she's never done this before. It's not like she hasn't spent a lifetime looking back at these eyes, the same longing gaze emanating from a thousand puppy eyes in five hundred hopeful heads. And he is sweet. And he does smile at her. And she doesn't recall him being obnoxious at all during their few contacts. And that's about the best a girl like her can hope for, and she lifts her head a tad, boosted with a smile of recognition: old friends. And he sure as hell caught that one! And he looks away so as not to spoil it: a hand darting back from a house of cards. And that's what we call encouragement.

Back on stage, and Sylvia must be spending too much time in front of one customer; the other men along the rail are looking beyond her to the table dancers, and even the guy she's with keeps stealing glimpses of Candy, who is off to his left, preoccupied with something on her slipper. The cocktail waitress whom Carroll saw for the first time Tuesday night is on tonight. She has to squeeze her way between two guys wearing name tags and fooling with a calculator to get to him, and her attitude as she takes his order betrays her suspicion that this is somehow part of his grand stratagem to stiff her. Sparkling apple cider may be delayed. He watches Sylvia conclude her set without major incident. The night is young. There's no point in avoiding it, this ineluctable conclusion, he'll have to ask

Stevie for a table dance tonight. No big deal, he's done it before. She's pretty busy, popular around here, and it may be the only way to have a private conversation with her. Could be she's even waiting for him to ask. Can't suggest it herself to him (violation of club rules). Best loosen up first though, get some cider in him, drop some singles on the rail—good way to find the groove.

He's got three, singles after counting, three. Sylvia has yet to reappear to collect her tips, so he slips out of his seat and puts one on the rail. Maybe a bit late, impulsive, but it's up there now and he's back in his seat. Cocktail waitress will be sure to give him his change in ones, so there's no anticipated shortage tonight. Sylvia comes out—still naked, and that's still strange—and collects her tips. She obviously doesn't want to do it, and she keeps her thank-yous to a minimum, not even looking up or trying to guess at the source of Carroll's tip. Water over the dam. Candy, presumably satisfied with the condition of her slipper, braces the corner of the bar along with Tamara, who is presumably satisfied with the condition of Tasha, still in the dressing area, presumably. Beyond them he spots the cocktail waitress, quiescently inspecting her nails in blithe disregard of the sweating bottle of sparkling apple cider and the glass of liquefying ice cubes on her tray. A changing state of matter, and now the barmaid's got a story to tell. Cocktail leans in, something else that Carroll won't hear.

All of a sudden someone is in front of him, all smiles: "Hi. My name is Andrea, and tonight is my first night here at Indiscretions. (a pause to let that sink in) I just wanted to take this opportunity to meet some of the customers and to say that I hope you'll stick around for a while (pause) and watch me dance." She gives her head a little bob, and she is on to the next guy.

Wow. Never has a dancer gone around and introduced herself like that before. He can hear her next to him, two guys at once this time: "Hi. My name is Andrea and tonight. . . ." Is this a new club policy, or is it, more likely considering the delivery, her own personal policy? Won't know for sure until she dances. You can always tell when a girl has danced on a lot of different stages and is getting used to a new one. Not that that'll prove anything. Okay, so that's Andrea. It's getting so he can't keep track anymore. It's getting so he doesn't know if he should. Let's see: very slender fashion-model look, brown hair and olive skin, slight European accent but impossible to be more specific just hearing that sales pitch (makes him want to buy more clothes), and he wouldn't know the difference anyway. Okay, so that's Andrea.

Back at the bar Candy and Tamara are laughing uncontrollably. The cocktail waitress finally picks up her tray, his the only order on it, and heads toward him. As soon as he spots her she looks at him. She glowers; she probably thinks he's been watching her the whole time. Special trip, that won't help, he thinks. This place is packed; how could it be that her tray isn't loaded with drinks? Here she comes. Should he talk first? Here she comes. Let her. This is nuts; what did he do? Where did this problem come from? He's a problem magnet. People look at him and right away they don't like him, want to make trouble for him, like that fat fuck corporate partner. Not Stevie though. She's like a window to a nicer place.

"Sparkling cider?" She says it real snidely, like it's a Shirley Temple with double cherry and this is an Old

West saloon. Never mind that they don't serve alcohol in here even if he wanted it. "Three-fifty," like he doesn't have it.

He was ready for her, and he proffers a ten, which rather than take from his hand, she just stares at, moving her tray directly below it and presumably waiting for him to drop it, as if not wanting to even touch a thing that he is also touching. Released from his fingers, the bill floats down to the tray. Cocktail clicks open her plastic change box and files the bill in the clipped lid section under Tens, withdraws six ones; two quarters come from the partitioned wells in the base of the box. She places his change in a roughly fanned stack and nudges the tray at him: your move. He picks up the six ones, leaving the quarters, as he sometimes does, for her. This should be no problem; he happens to know that a lot of guys take the quarters too. Those guys want to save all their tipping for the dancers, but Carroll knows that the cocktail waitresses work hard around here.

"You forgot your quarters, Mr. Trump," she sneers. Now the hand's on the hip. She feels it should be there.

He doesn't know what to say. He knows he's being insulted, but he isn't quick enough to formulate a response that she won't be able to use against him—this much he can see.

"They're for you," he tries, forcing himself to meet her eye. He's in a conflict, and he doesn't want to shy away, doesn't want this girl to sow false seed about him in Stevie's garden. "I think it's fair," he adds, seeing that she's not satisfied with *they're for you*. "It's what I usually tip when I get a drink. I know you're pretty new here, and I hope this is enough for you. None of the other girls ever said anything about it." Further than he meant to go, but the ball was rolling.

Her expression doesn't change, not that he can see. "Yeah. Right. Thanks. Forget it," she says. Hand leaves hip, and she splits.

Wondering if Stevie saw the exchange, he looks around the place. A little shaky, he'd sure feel better if he could garner her approval, a nod, a reassuring smile. She's a sharp cookie and would probably know by now that this waitress is difficult. If she noticed them talking she might have taken an interest and watched closely. He's sure she'd be on his side. But he can't find her. She must have slipped into the ladies' room, or maybe into the dressing area. Maybe she'll be dancing next. In any case she's not in the room, and he doubts that she witnessed his conversation with the cocktail waitress. It did happen pretty quick, and she is a busy girl.

The DJ/doorman announces Candy. How'd she get up there so fast? Seems like she was just down here talking at the bar. Maybe the thing with the waitress wasn't that quick after all. Candy's routine is not exactly innovative. Pretty standard fare. He'd rather have Stevie up there right now. Give him a chance to stare at her without it seeming awkward. Give him a chance to tip her, maybe another thank you. Maybe she'd wink at him, smile, or be facing him when she removes her top. Any kind of interaction would be great. It would give him a chance to figure out what the best way to reach her is. He really wants to talk to her, wants to foster their relationship. Just to make a move, like with Solo, is important, and it could lead to . . . coffee tonight after work? a phone number? He craves some forward motion here (not a conclusion, doesn't have to be anywhere near a conclusion). He learned that at the office this week. It would have been great to find Solo, and he'll find it next week, but just looking and acting beyond the parameters of prayer was in itself a reward, like a carrot on a stick, maybe, worst case, a great big con. Yet the cart gets pulled, and the carrot, at least, doesn't get any farther away. Candy's okay, just another pretty girl taking off her clothes for him. Face it: how much of this can you really look at?

"Everything," says a woman's voice, spent and from the booths behind him, not really loud and only clear to him because he's so close.

He turns to look. It's Tasha, that girl who was gone for a while, giving a table dance to some stiff. She's got her leg up on one end of the hinged counter that drops down over the customer's lap once he is seated. This counter is evidently for the dancer's protection, but Tasha uses it to her advantage. Her panties, from this angle, look to be held back by her left hand, close to her raised thigh and off her crotch. Other leg meets solid ground, and the stiff is getting an eyeful of How Tasha Works. For this demonstration her breasts, the usual objects of a table dance, have been superseded by this, her nexus, a more urgent matter, and her right hand is the guide, combing, exploring, opening Stiff's eyes and mind to these troubled tender waters. Stiff tries hard. He is . . . uncertain of his response.

Carroll can see the guy through her parted legs, the way his head sinks on his shoulder, ever lower, peering into Tasha's pussy, trying hard to see into her cunt, like there's an answer in there, an answer that he needs right now. Carroll hates this guy. Tasha, her digital encouragement notwithstanding, doesn't appear too enamored of him either. She drops her shoulders and lets out a sigh, moves her right hand to her right buttock.

"Here," she says with thinly veiled disillusionment, "you do it. I've had enough." So she stands, legs parted, cynically proffered.

Like that until the song ends. Tasha backs away, Stiff bails, she to the ladies' room, he to greener pastures. Carroll returns to Candy. Candy returns to the dressing area.

Stevie, whence unclear, crosses the room. Always around somewhere, a girl like this, who isn't? Dead guys, that's who. Silly now, but it looks like she's walking toward him, and he looks away rather than appear the expectant fool. But you'll never guess what. . . .

"Hi. How are you doing?" she says. Chipper. To her it's another moment, here we go on another any-old moment. "That's a great shirt, I wanted to come over and tell you. Is it new?" Funny, but the shirt really does look kind of nice, she thinks.

He yanks his eyes from the sparkling apple cider before him, sticky stuff, and manages Stevie's chin. "Yes, I just bought it today." Pulling a fold of sleeve for her inspection: "See, there are black curlicues on the black fabric. I don't know if you can see—the light has to be right— but they're there." He stays with the sleeve for a beat, then returns to her chin but diffidently drops to her neck, looking at her neck, depriving himself of her angel eyes, penance for a weak demonstration. He's a poor source of entertainment. Want fun? Look elsewhere.

"Oh yes, I see," she says. She loves this guy. Why can't all men be this sweet? Of course that could get dreary . . . okay, half the men? Well some men anyhow. Some men should be this sweet. Time to go. "Well . . . I'm glad to see you made it in tonight. I hope you'll stick around and watch me dance."

Can't just let her leave. Look at her eyes. "Oh yes, I came to see you dance. I came to see *you* dance. When will you be on?" And he interrupts before she can get an answer out: "Not that it matters. Anytime's fine, you know. I'll be here all night, so I'll see you whenever you go on." Now he's at her eyes. It's going okay.

"Actually I'm on right after Candy." Puppy. "Next. As a matter of fact I was heading over there to get ready when I saw you."

Carroll thinks, What about before? Didn't you see me before? "I'll be here," he says optimistically, indicating his chair. Then, worried that she might think him cheap, a sit-off-the-stage-so-you-can-dodge-the-tips freeloader, he adds, "I like to sit on the stage. I *would* sit on the stage, especially to see you dance, but there's no place to sit there. (an arm outstretched, more demonstration) It's pretty crowded."

Yes, yes, little puppy. I know you're not trying to stiff me. "Yes, they do a good business here, don't they? Well I gotta run, maybe I'll see you a little later." She sees that he still looks worried. Better let him know that I don't think he's trying to stiff me. "Hey, and thanks again for the table dance the other night." Was it one or two? "That was very nice of you. I had a good time." She's gone, perpetual motion.

"Bye," he gets out, and in time because she waves backward to him without turning around: gotta run.

He tries to watch Candy, but he can't keep his eyes from the curtain that leads to the dressing area. It might swing open, part in response to a bump or a breeze, and reveal a glimpse of Stevie. He'd like to see that, catch her alone, doing something common like pulling off a sock-stocking. It would be a way to understand better, a window to who she is and what she thinks of things. We can be sure of this much: she likes him. Really, this is quite a coup. Ground has been covered well. He evidently has a knack for this. Something clicks. She's in control, where he feels she should be. There's a dynamic at work here that he had better get a hold of. As with Solo, this is no time to procrastinate. He doubts he could even if he had a choice. Best watch her dance, refrain from tipping as a way to further separate himself from the pack, but ask for a table dance as soon as she's done. Give her a chance to catch her breath, then ask for a table dance, a *table*. Seems like you'd call it just a table for short, seems like if the dancers were talking among themselves they'd call it a table. Candy leaves the stage. DJ/doorman informs those in attendance that that was her third of three and that a lovelylady by the name of Stevie will be out next for the first of three. As Candy returns to collect her tips the curtain does indeed swing open long enough for Carroll to witness a flash of flesh and blond hair. Beautiful. Candy looks happy picking up her money. She did well with this set. DJ/doorman is watching her too, no music on right now so he capriciously spins a knob on the lighting console. Things red in the room turn black, and Carroll looks up. Could've guessed: all the lights are green.

Then lots of colors. Click go the moments and she is there, pretty dancer, pretty girl, pretty person (very person). Easy stuff for her, but Carroll can hear his heartbeat, feel the blood in his veins, like you're not there yet but here's a reason to keep on. For this first she wears. . . . But all details smack unworthy of description in the light of What Stevie Is. They are so many notes to the music, pixels on the screen, trees in the forest . . . no, less than that, they are shadowy contributors, not participants. She is a singular thing amidst a group of witnesses, a starlet surrounded by leering executive producers. Carroll's old Vega is sitting out there in the lot, cloaked in darkness and, one can't help but wonder even in this paradise called Southern California especially if one has ever been in the dark and blighted cities of the East, perhaps a modicum of rust. Maybe? Unobserved in the deepest corners of the farthest reaches of a blueprint maze, visited maybe once by a graphite explorer traveling across the Plane of Draft Table, an intrepid mouse cursor lost in a jungle of icons, a CADscape? That rust, say in a shock tower, got there by itself. Innocent steel now in the throes of metamorphosis, like coal to crystal, something from something else, a long, slow screw. Click goes the mouse. There are hands at the ends of those things, and lots of colors.

Think about Candy: now there's a girl he's seen naked many times, and while it may not be as thrilling as it once was to him, when she took her clothes off tonight she was still a naked girl. This is true of all the dancers he's ever seen. The thrill of seeing them naked moves along a downward slope, diminishing as the number of times he sees them increases. Of course there are minor glitches, jumps in the graph, but generally that's how it works around here. Stevie's not like that. Though compared to how much time he's spent watching most of the other girls he's only seen her dance a few times, he is familiar enough with the program to know that she's different, so very clearly, so elementally different. Not something he ever expected to show up on this stage. It's no longer three of three to him; it's one of one, amorphous segments of time that hold her before him, brief lapses that go unnoticed by him, caught in rapturous recollection of the vision, the one just now gone away, by her too, caught in the celeritous moves that lead her from song to song, from naked to more naked, from dealer to dealt.

This set is over for the room. For Carroll it lingers slickerly, saliva stretching mouth to mouth at the close of a deep and tangled kiss. But no, truth is Stevie's done, back in the dressing area wrapping her ass in lace.

"Stevie, gentlemen. Put your hands together for the lovely Stevie. Don't forget, gentlemen, topless table dances are available from any one of our lovelyladies . . . including our next lovelylady . . . (papers ruffle). They're up close and personal, so be sure to ask. . . . The lovely Andrea, gentlemen. Coming up next is our newest lovelylady—I know some of you have met her already—newest . . . by the name of Andrea." DJ/doorman gives it a rest.

Carroll's really very preoccupied with Stevie, more so even than in nights past. This new girl, while quite nice, potential dream material if you think about it, just can't manage to steal his mind away. Sure, he watches as she takes the stage, one click more concerned with her routine than the other girls with theirs, than even she will be in precious few days to come, aimin' to please on this her first night, if not her first set. Watches, yes, but his heart's not in it. Like when he was a kid home alone and Mom was out on a date. She'd always promise to be home at a certain hour, and she would always be late. That gap, the difference between promised and actual, never failed to plunge him into terror and trepidation. Dad had gone way south, like dead, during one of his own missed deadlines, and that put it beyond him to count on the fact that Mom, though always late, eventually did return. Always had, without fail. Still, it was all just so much rationalization, not much help when the clock was ticking and she was late and he was alone watching the clock tick her into later still. Special treat: watch past-bedtime programs with impunity! Watch them, sure. Look at them, more like. There was no way he could follow them, much less enjoy them, with Mom out past *her* bedtime. He didn't think this far into it back then, but of course the irony is that there was also no way he could watch them at all when she was home on time. Yeah, Andrea is way hot. Too bad he can't follow. He just can't follow.

The curtain didn't close completely (it rarely does, she's noticed, just like every place she's worked, and isn't that funny? like they view this all as work, being naked, being naked on their time, whatever context: work), and Stevie can see this girl Andrea out there giving it her all. Looks better than me, she thinks.

Candy, lingering back here like she's never gonna leave, nudges Stevie's elbow with a soiled slipper and says, "Look at this. What do you suppose this is? Gum? It wasn't there when I came in tonight."

Dressing in privacy is a rare treat when working, and it doesn't look like it's going to happen tonight. She glances at the slipper but doesn't really see anything on it. "Gum, I guess," she says.

Candy sets her mouth: I knew it. Ready to see gum more than ever now, she pulls back the slipper: gum. "Well how do I get it out?" she wants to know.

Jeez, that Andrea's got a swell ass. Did I ever look that
good? What is it? Lighter fluid? Or will that ruin the fabric? Oh hell, better see if it really is gum before I start giving advice. Always like this, no shortcuts, no way to even
pull your fucking panties on without an audience.

"Lemme see again," says Stevie, and Candy deferen-
tially hands her the slipper. "This here? This little spot?"
It's a tiny, crusty dot, right over the big toe.

Candy nods solemnly: what do we do now?

Stevie casts about for a knife, finds a nail file sticking out of a makeup pouch bearing the legend EVA let-
tered with a laundry marker like for kids at camp, and
flicks off the offending matter with two strokes. "There
you go," she says, handing the slipper back. Who the hell
is Eva?

Thank-yous are interrupted by Andrea, who is between songs. This girl's really darling, and young, and
Stevie hasn't even been here a week, and now she'll be
banished to the periphery of attention. Did I ever look like
that? Brand new, a perfect image, a mirror.

"Hiya!" sparkles Andrea. She's what Stevie's boyfriend would call a nice piece of work.

. . . work, or sometime during the day if that's too late.
Maybe she's off tomorrow. Okay, he doesn't want to get
ahead of himself. First things first, and first thing is a table
dance. Carroll watches the curtain, the side one, the one
that Stevie will eventually, if she ever finishes dressing,
come out of. Not the stage curtain, the one that new
Andrea will come out of for her second of three.

And come out they do, both of them in fact, out of
their respective curtains. For some reason Stevie looks a
little distressed all of a sudden, and maybe it would be

prudent to wait and not ask for a table dance right this minute. Andrea looks great to those who have an eye for her, not to mention genuinely pleased to be naked. Something may be missing there though. She takes her clothes off as if it were a conclusion instead of an implication, like if the attention of one of the guys along the rail got too graphic, too lecherous and to the point, she would be bewildered. This is all lost on Carroll, who is consumed with anxiety about how best to time his table dance request, though it helps to get another look at Stevie's face, already relaxing into laughter with some guy at the rear counter. Nice how she's so friendly to everybody, even these jerks.

Cocktail is here, emptying the balance of his cider from bottle to glass. "Ready for more?" she accuses.

"I guess . . . sure," he says, eyes more on Stevie than on her. Sudden resolve. "Here, I'll pay you now. I need to go to the men's room."

She doesn't like this one bit but takes the money. What can she do? The guy's in here all the time. And what does he think he's staring at over there? "Do this," she says, placing a cocktail napkin on top of his glass. "People will know that you're still here." Then, annoyed at the fact that he is still preoccupied and evidently ungrateful for her instruction: "This is what you do everywhere when you're leaving your drink for a minute. Haven't you ever been in a bar?" She storms off without waiting for an answer.

And Carroll, though he always *has* wondered why some drinks have napkins on top of them, is far too uptight to ponder that now. Plan to walk right by her. If there's any way to talk then talk, if not go to the rest room, maybe try again on the return trip. He walks in her direction while looking mostly toward the men's room, ostensibly taking this slightly-out-of-the-way way to avoid the crowd around the stage. Almost to her, six feet, and it looks like he'll have to pass her by as she's still involved in her conversation. Right next to her, chance a toward glance, slap on a pleasant howyadoin grin . . . and just then she looks up. They're virtually nose to nose. Oh, serendipity! and no time to think.

"Could you do a table . . . ?" (wants to add "dance" but it gets choked off and he ends up sounding that much cooler like he's mastered the jargon of the place and of the girls, who, as he suspected, really do refer to table dances as *tables*)

"Sure . . ." (wants to add his name but can't remember it or if she even knows it so the inflection that would normally segue into the direct address is left hanging for a beat and almost sounds to him at least like enthusiasm)

"I'll be over at my seat. Just ask for Carroll." (wants this to sound witty and is completely unaware of how propitious it was for him to choose this moment to inadvertently remind her of his name)

"Okay, I'll be right over." (wants to use his name now that she has it but is always sensitive to these situations and doesn't want to sound like she's using it just because she's relieved to be given it when she maybe should have known it all along)

Carroll makes a beeline back to his seat, forgetting that he was on his way to the men's room. Stevie turns to the man she was speaking with and excuses herself, forgetting his name too. On the stage Andrea is done with her set, but before passing into the dressing area she bends forward and moons the room.

"Thank you, everybody," she lilts.

At his seat, mouth dry and palms wet, the room becomes more something he's watching than something he's sitting in. His mom could do that too. He'd be sitting on the sofa watching TV, and she'd switch on the vacuum cleaner in the hallway. Then the noise was a player, looming, growing louder, already competing strongly with the television. Remotes weren't around yet, and the living room floor, where he and the TV were, collected its share of cookie crumbs, so things would only get worse. Ever louder. All of a sudden he wasn't a kid watching television in a living room; now he was a kid watching a room in which a television set was on. It comes and goes and goes and comes. To him, at that age, there were plenty more cookies yet to be eaten, sans saucer, but Mom and Hoover could always fix that. There is a way to tell, out of the corner of your eye, how she's—Stevie that is, in the here and now—how she's killing time: look at her hands, they never quite complete any of the many tiny gestures that they begin. Now we're killing time until the moments prior to the start of the next song. Table dance punctuation, he learned from last time. There's a girl on stage. It's someone he knows, but that's as far as it goes. Like groggily trying to prepare the coffeemaker too soon after crawling out of bed, you look at the parts, you know they belong there, but you really can't identify them beyond that. Your mind isn't ready, but Stevie is. Why else would she walk toward him and look at him, both at the same time?

She's here. "Are we ready," she says. This won't be so bad, she thinks, and for the first time she realizes that a guy like Carroll, all the guys like Carroll, aren't all that bad, could in fact compare favorably to her boyfriend (that fuck). Makes her think of when she's so sick of the music here that she could bust and the barmaid turns on the mixer to make a milk shake for the fat manager so he can get even fatter (like that'll help his case when he wants to walk her out to the car at night) and the noise drowns out the music for a few seconds, and it's a relief. That stupid buzzing mixer, for those few seconds, sounds better than the music. She can tell by looking at Carroll that he has a little extra money tonight. Better pace the conversation; he's probably looking for more than one or two songs to-night. Guess three. Four. A few.

At her direction he climbs into a booth. She follows and drops the counter over his lap. Surprisingly she mut-ters an embarrassed apology about this—surprising be-cause every other dancer, including her every other time, gets through this tricky moment by acting as if it were a natural adjunct to being seated anywhere: there we go. Carroll doesn't mind but lets it go without comment. He thinks the counter will give him a place to put his hands, but he ends up keeping them in his lap, at the ends of his arms.

"Comfy?" she wants to know once he is seated.

"Indeed," he says suavely. *Indeed?* he thinks.

She gets top-naked in short order and makes it to the song just a second or two after it begins. This guy . . . Carroll . . . this guy Carroll isn't really such a bad way to spend a few minutes, she thinks. One look around the place tells her that, and she wants to give him his money's worth. Whatever that is, his money's worth. Funny how much bread guys will pay just to look at her tits. She's been taking it for so long that it almost seems natural; in fact, natural may be exactly what it is. Still it's weird. It's not

like they can touch her or anything, and when she acci-
dentally touches them, say brushes a nose with a nipple,
well that happens so infrequently that they can't possibly
be hoping for that. And even that, what's in that?

He loves looking at her breasts. So close, what could
be better? He's seen enough of her now—not to imply that
he's used to it, that would be ridiculous—that he has
grown somewhat familiar with her body. This is his second time in a booth with her, two songs the last time, and
he feels that they are sharing something. She knows that
he's looking at her breasts. Sometimes she even looks at
them while he's looking at them. It's something they're
doing together. There's an attachment, he knows there is,
he can feel it. She's beautiful. This is different from anything anywhere. It's sex. It's better than you can imagine.
When she's on stage he can only watch her, but here in
the booth alone with her he can touch her with his eyes.
It's sex. It's enough.

"So what do you do, Carroll? How does a guy make
enough money to afford such nice clothes?" This last intended as a friendly but facetious little allusion to their
earlier conversation. But pass it by, not a great kidder. No
harm though. He'll probably just take it as a compliment—
and why not? They are nice clothes.

He blushes, cheeks fire tickle-red before those cool
and neutral breasts. "I sort of splurged . . . but I can't
afford to do it very often. I'm a file clerk at a law firm. Been
doing it forever, but they still don't pay me all that much.
Head file clerk, actually." And, as if in apology for going
with *head* file clerk, he adds, "You can only go so far."

She can see he feels humbled and ashamed at this
latter admission, and she knows he shouldn't be, maybe

even wouldn't be if it weren't for her standing here naked, waiting to be impressed. "Yeah," she says, "well that sounds fine, Carroll. (lower, firmer tone: oral parentheses) Turns out you can only get so naked, too."

She holds his eye for a beat: why not. She feels liquid in the heat: see what I've got. The music spins her 'round to the room. The base smacks her ass with its boom. But there ain't much to see out there, and there'll be even less tomorrow. She'd like to crawl into the booth with Carroll and sit down right next to him, order some fries and hear all about file clerking. But that won't happen; with the counter down she can hardly get her feet into boothspace and out of roomspace. Instead she arches backward, leans all the way back until her nipples point skyward and her cheek is next to his cheek and they're both looking down over the implacable topography of her chest.

"That was nice," Carroll says after she turns back around and is facing him. For the life of him he couldn't find a thing to say while he was at her cheek, and now that he's finally commented his voice sounds stupid to him, the words inadequate.

"Good," says Stevie. It was nice. "I don't think my boss would like it though." She shoots a conspiring glance, smile.

And if she were less sincere or he sharper, he might view that remark as a ploy: c'mon we're on the same side so let's open your wallet and share the wealth. But they aren't and it isn't. "You're not supposed to do that?" he asks.

"I'm not supposed to be 'overly intimate,' they tell us. To you I'm supposed to look like I'm having the time of my life, but to them and the other customers I'm supposed to look like I'm waiting for someone more exciting to dance for. They told me this when I auditioned. I don't know what it means, but if you look when a girl dances . . . (waits for him to catch up, then on his nod) she'll a lot of times drop her smile when she turns away from the booth."

"I guess I've noticed that, but I've never really thought about it," he says, fascinated to be having this conversation, amazed that he could talk to any girl like this and more amazed that he could talk so easily to this girl about anything. It's as if they've known each other for a long time—but even that would be new to him. Maybe it's like she's a person he always knew and just started talking with, like himself at home, or the television. It's like talking to himself and the television. He feels safe. "Could I ask you something? I notice sometimes . . . about table dances? Could I ask you?" Like go ahead. Like pull away. Like turn up the volume.

"Sure," she says lightly. She's down on her haunches, hands on the counter, barely swaying to the waning notes of the song. Familiar but better. "Sounds like our song's almost over. We can do another, or if you want to save some money we can talk at your seat, but I may not be able to stand there too long." This sounds bad. "I mean there may be other guys asking me for a table." She nods her head a few times rapidly: my hands are tied. She wouldn't mind if he took another dance. That wouldn't be so bad. It's a nice break. He's a sweet guy.

"Oh, another!" Relax. "I've got plenty of money tonight—I don't mean to brag, just so you know it's okay. Please stay. I'd like another." In his excitement he moves his hands to the top of the counter, gripping, something to hold on to the way he wants to hold the moment.

"Good, that's great, I'd like to stay." *Plenty of money,* she thinks. Sweet. Just hope you never really do have

plenty of money. I bet it's easier than that, I bet you don't
even want *plenty of money.* I bet you're a safe bet. I bet
you're okay. She wants him to understand, "I'm sorry,
about the money, but they watch and they count—"

"It's okay, really. I know, I understand, I know," he
interrupts. Even turns his palms out in a matching gesture, but drops them quickly back to the counter when he
realizes how close they are to her breasts. He reddens, not
much, it goes away. She understands too.

The next song is picking up, but they barely notice
it. "What did you want to ask me?" she says.

He remembers. It should be okay. "Sometimes when
I'm watching the table dances from across the room . . .
(eyes wide, waits for her nod), sometimes it looks like the
dancer dips so far into the booth that she must be touching the guy . . . you know . . . with her front. (encouraged
by her grin) I'm sure she isn't. It's just that it looks that
way from back there." (nod at the room behind Stevie)
He's unsure of how to wrap up his question; it sounds to
him like he didn't really ask anything at all. "So I was just
wondering: do the dancers ever touch the customers?"

"Not allowed," she says, still grinning at his word
front. "And why would we want to? It would have to be
someone—at least for me—it would have to be someone
that I really liked." And she rises with the building music,
leans into the booth, and gives a touch of a nipple to the
tip of his nose. "Like a friend," she adds, withdrawing to
a more standard posture, swaying back into the general
beat of the music that fills the general place.

A nipple to the nose would normally incapacitate
Carroll, but in the context of this already overwhelming
situation he manages to roll with it, file it for later prayer-

ful collapse on his bed. This is wonderful. This makes up for everything. "I bet you have a lot of friends," he says, innocently following.

Didn't her boyfriend accuse her of this not long ago, the jerk? But she knows this is not a snide remark coming from Carroll. Does she have a lot of friends? "No, not really. Other strippers. But they're not friends, not really," she answers, lips pursed: answer in progress. Keeping in policy and keeping mostly in motion, she sweeps his face with her hair. Does she want a lot of friends? "You?" she asks.

"No. Are you kidding? I talk to people at work, but I never see them after. I feel funny with people (not you). Sometimes. . . . I don't know (you). Nobody (you)." He'd give anything to be frozen in the moment forever with her, like maybe a *Twilight Zone* thing, or an old *Bewitched* where Samantha freezes the humans so she can fix what ever trouble Endora's stirred up. Always sounded neat, only now Carroll wants to be one of the frozen ones. Let Samantha take care of business.

"They like us to keep moving," Stevie explains as she turns and beats out a sway or two in reverse. Then around and back on her haunches: "I know what you mean. It's nice to spend time alone."

He knows he should do something, say something. Maybe too soon now, but eventually he'll be out of money and there'll be no more table dances. Of course they're friends now—she pretty much said so—and he doesn't want to spoil the mood. Can't risk scaring her away. So new at this, so much to know. Be casual. He says, "Do you have a boyfriend?"

No. "Yeah," she says dejectedly, as if she were responding to *Do you have a lot of homework to do tonight?*

"Part-time, you could say." Then after some quick consideration: "He's okay, I've known him for a while." Final word. That's it. Resolved. "You?" she asks, hopes yes, hopes no.

"Are you kidding?" *Are you kidding?* didn't he just say that? "I mean, no. I mean, girls don't seem to like me. I mean, I haven't met anybody yet. Once I saw a movie with a girl in high school, then we had lunch the next day. It was sort of an assignment. The movie, I mean."

"What movie was it?" she asks, because she has to say something, because she has to confirm for him that it was all right to mention this, because she has to let him know that if this is the best he can come up with for a romantic history, then it's good enough for her.

He concentrates, but it won't help. "I don't remember. Some French thing. See, that was the assignment—it was for French class—to understand this movie. I didn't. I wasn't where you were supposed to be in the class. I could never understand any of the language. She told me after it. The girl told me what it was called in English, but it was too late and I didn't care. It was black and white. It was people in dark rooms saying things to each other that made no sense to me. I guess now I would be able to rent it in English and cheat. But you couldn't rent movies then. You had to be . . . you know . . . (he looks around the small booth as if therein lies the word he is seeking). Clever! that's it. You had to be clever to cheat then. I'm not clever."

The second song is winding down. She taps his hand twice with her fingers, then leaves them resting there, in contact.

He gets it. "Could we do another? Do you have time for another?" The feel of her fingers on the back of his hand, it's wonderful.

Glad to be in one of those effortless little conversations that spring up out of nowhere in the oddest places, she is. "Absolutely," she says. "Gotta tell you that this'll be three, just so you know." Off his nod she rises, silence between songs now, and straightens her panties. She's done fives before. Five's about the limit. It is the limit technically, and it's about the most you can do and still have time to catch your breath before your next set. Of course five songs can be endless with most of the customers who have the bread to blow like that. Catch twenty-two. Catch two-two. Catch too-too. This is nice, hardly ever get five out of a guy you don't mind talking with. Even if it stays only three—but guessing five—nice.

Their third song begins. Stevie rises and does some standard dipping, breast swinging ultra close to Carroll, and really, because she knows that he won't do anything out of line, her attitude is: anything goes. She's right, right? Stay true to form. He's a good boy, smart enough to know that sometimes one has to preserve the future, the five-minute future. A new trick for him, this easy talk down a two-way street, yet he apprehends the gossamer fabric of it all, the way it can be savored but not bitten, the way it can't be forced, the way it will always be his, the way it will metamorphose into a precious memory, the way her diaphanous panties cling to her skin like breath on a mirror. For want of protection it isn't enough.

Not a thought, but quicker, as say a flash is, his hand, make it the first three fingers of his right, turn upward and stroke once the side and underside of her left breast, three o'clock to fivethirtynine. It isn't enough.

She's cool enough that she doesn't pull away but merely puts some inner defense mechanism back on alert, where it should be kept anyhow when dancing this close to a customer. Carroll evidently had one credit and used it up. They both sense this immediately, and he will not lift those fingers again.

His face reddens. The words come hard but come they must. "I . . . I'm sorry. I . . . I wasn't thinking. I—"

"Forget it," she cuts him off with. "Just. . . . We can't do that." She's patient but strained, like talking to someone else's child with that someone else in the room. She's also a little sorry that he did it, and she wants to believe that it was just a glitch, wants to believe that she never lets anybody do that, no matter who they are or how much bread they're flashing. A glitch.

Though it is still early in this, their third song, he feels things slipping and wants her to know that everything's all right. "I want two more songs after this," he blurts out optimistically, hoping that this assurance will somehow make things all better. "If it's okay with you. I promise I won't do that again. I want to stay here as long as I can. I'm sorry. I promise I won't do that again." He nods his head rapidly: see, it's all better now.

"All right," she says, because she has to, and because she hopes they'll recover so that he can leave tonight feeling good. "That'll be five total, and I'm afraid that that's the most we can do in one stretch."

"It's the most I can afford," he says frankly.

That helps her some, but not enough. It's gone, and it confounds her to be so very at the whim of a learned response that probably doesn't apply here at all. That touch, that stupid little forward motion performed so innocently, sent him hurling back to the moon. Wonder if he'll spot it someday, figure it out or find it in a dream? If so he'll be better off than she. They walk through two and a half songs, she making perfunctory conversation and showing him her ass more than anything else, even pulling aside her panties and daring herself to push up close to his face, he doing his best to be agreeably responsive, to fool both of them into thinking that these latter dances are every bit as fine as the first ones were. Stevie mourns the lost communication. She enjoyed it as much as he did. But she knows you can't make that stuff happen. You can only be there while it happens on its own. There's no real control. You can pull aside your panties, but there's no real control. She can't help him. She can't help her. She's not God.

Sundaymonday

N othing's worse than having a chore to do on
Sunday, and after what happened last night,
him blowing it with Stevie, he especially
doesn't want to even get out of bed, much less drive all
the way down to San Pedro to go to his cousin Adam's
wedding. Think about the hours of anxiety you poured
into this day during the weeks since receiving the invitation, and how it all just vanished when Stevie danced into
your life. All that anxiety and worry about going to this
wedding, all for nothing. Seems like by forgetting it for a
few days he made it all go to waste, the anxiety, like it
never happened or doesn't mean anything, and now he's

gotta go to this wedding without having enough time to fret over it. Sounds silly, but he can't help feeling cheated. This is cousin Adam whom he hasn't seen in what seems like (and probably is) years, cousin Adam who is some nth cousin on his father's side and who wouldn't have even invited Carroll but for the fact that he's the only living relative in Los Angeles, and more to the point, he's a warm body to help occupy Adam's plenty-of-elbow-room side of the boat—they're getting married on a boat—so it'll balance with the bride's could-you-squeeze-in-a-little-tighter side. *We really need you,* Adam wrote in pen on the bottom of the invitation. A boat. Probably shouldn't go, just stay here in bed and let them all sink, listing to port.

He killed himself last night. That's what he did when he touched Stevie's breast. He killed himself, and now he's just a soulless corpse, a walking bag of bones. Why not go and sit on the boat? Dead is dead, what does he care where he does it? All that's left now is to wait the forty or so years it will take for his body to catch up to his spirit. Then everyone else will know he's dead. For now it's just him. And Stevie. Just he and Stevie know he's dead. He rolls out of bed and uses the toilet.

Punctuality is a priority, even in despondency. So he gets right out of there, which is just fine because looking at himself in the mirror is not working out too well. The invitation, evidently written with the Valley-born bride's family in mind, advises Valley-dwelling attendees to take either the 405 all the way down to the 110 or take the 101 (Ventura) to the 101 (Hollywood) to the 110 (Harbor not Pasadena). It's the 110 that's the key here. That will take you right into San Pedro, where you can follow the surface-street map drawn on the bottom to the big treasure-map **X**, drawn on the map next to the legend *You Found It!!!* Should be no problem, even if he does have to interpolate a west side jumping-on point in this Valley–to–San Pedro sequence. He needs to stop at the K'mon-n-Mart for a gift, so he decides on the 10 to the 110. But after slamming the Vega's hatch on a set of hastily-wrapped-in-the-parking-lot Corelle Livingware and merging onto the Santa Monica Freeway (or the 10 East), he suddenly gets so consumed with regret over not buying a friends-again? present for Stevie, like maybe that blue scarf that he couldn't get for the wedding cause it would've been just for the bride, that he misses the ramp for the 110 and finds himself passing downtown Los Angeles before he realizes his mistake. Fuck! Still driving, he pulls out his *Thomas Guide* and tries to glom clues during quick glances from the road ahead of him. Okay, okay: how 'bout the—what is it? the 710? the Long Beach?—yeah. Take the 710. . . . No, no, take the 5 . . . the 60 . . . 5 is better. Take the 5 to the 710 to the 91 back to the 110. Better than turning around at this point. Should be no problem.

Think about Garden Grove, one of a million places that Carroll has never been. Sometimes the only way to get to a place is to be going to a different place; then that goes wrong and there you are. Or just start in Los Angeles, pick the wrong thread, and *poof,* no wedding. White steel, silver glass: The Crystal Cathedral, a massive star-shaped tower he saw at wit's end while driving aimlessly around Garden Grove. Prodigious, yet in a way that's less soaring and more stunningly spread out: God's nose after a long and full boxing career. Carroll and the Vega are parked there now, Adam's wedding probably already over, somewhere far away. He'll never know where; he'll be lucky if he ever gets back home.

Turns out that unless you're clairvoyant there's no way to be ready for the 710 connecting ramp when it suddenly appears on the 5 at fifty-five miles per hour, and it doesn't help that everyone else speeds like hell and never mind that it's Sunday they come up behind him like they want to drive right through him then flash their lights when he's as far to the left as he can be. He opted then for the 605 with the unlikely notion of taking it to the 405 and backtracking to the 110, but ended up on the 22 going east not west, finally exited at random, wandered till he saw the tower. It was a place to go that you could get to by sight. Good enough for now.

Two ninety-foot doors are parted before him. Part of the cathedral's design, this, to let the service spill out over the parking lot and touch those who don't wish to leave their automotive sanctuary. The doors are a link to the first days of these same services in 1955, then held not far from here at a drive-in movie theater. Innovative gospel then, and today as well; Carroll can see the television cameras inside the cathedral capturing the video Word and passing it along to the waiting world. He's pretty sure he's breezed past this guy once or twice on a double-digit station between dueling phone-sex ads, robe of regal blue, bib sullied with on-screen call-in super, an 800 number, like it was a link to something bigger. And maybe it is. Carroll turns his car radio to the frequency indicated on the program he was handed as he pulled in, and the Word is given.

Not that he wants to hear it, not these spurious words. He turns down the volume and settles his head back on

the ripped vinyl headrest. Nearby a fountain plays. There's
the lightest of breezes, traffic on the street behind him. He
can't quite hear either the sermon or the splashes. The
sounds compete, but to him it's just a pleasant background
hum by which he can think. About Stevie. About what
guys at work would call *damage control*. He hates that.
Everything's gotta be jargon, a club, like those stupid old
lawyer cartoons they all love on their walls. They try to
be self-deprecating, but they really love themselves to
death. Still, it wouldn't be bad to be a part of *some* kind of
club. He lifts his head and looks at the cars around him.
Some are empty, some are packed with families. Most are
older couples, listening raptly to the radio, maybe holding—he can't really see—hands, trying to find a way to
do all this right. Face it: if the Word comes over a car radio
or a television, then car radios and TVs must be a-okay. If
angels dance at strip clubs, then we're all wearing too
much clothing.

He's changed lately, become more aggressive. His
renegade search for the SoLo/Bombgate file is one ex-
ample, his pawing of Stevie another, less happy one. But
for better or worse this is him. Think about how the more
you ask for the less you get, and sometimes, like with
Melissa and her dancing, the less you want something the
more you ask for it. None of this applies to Stevie, of course.
She walks above it all, a real angel, maybe just a person
like him but with finer tuning, grown beyond his confusion. A collective moan rises from the cars around him,
also over the radio and from within the cathedral. Not
really a moan, just sounds like that when you're not listening. These people are clearly impressed by whatever
it is they're hearing, and though he feels like an interloper

here he still can't bring himself to turn up the volume of his radio. Better to leave it all a hum than to risk disappointment. Better leave it alone, save the space for a surer bet. Another, stronger breeze sweeps the lot like a gift for those around him. He lifts his head again from the vinyl but in time only for the vacuum of its passage, and he feels like a kid watching Christmas gifts being opened at his parents' friends' house. There's nothing here for him. He wishes he would have paid more attention to the TV broadcast of this service when he passed by it those few times. Somewhere in the upper fifties, he thinks it was. It might make him want to listen now; at least it would be interesting to see it all from both sides, like the time he went to a taping of *Wheel of Fortune* in Burbank. So different. These guys pulling strings that the viewer doesn't even know about. You're just supposed to sit there with your Swanson dinner and give it your all, a sort of suspension of disbelief. Bet that fat fuck still has Solo. Bet he knows it. Bet it'll turn up one way or another soon. Tomorrow. Carroll will make it turn up. Wonder how he looks sitting in a booth at Indiscretions? He couldn't really tell from a glimpse he partly caught in that far mirror. Maybe he looks like all the other guys, like those chimpanzees he saw on television yesterday. The woman in the white coat, that would be Stevie. Another groaning noise. What is it these people hear? What does he have to do to hear the same thing? What does he have to not do? Turning up the radio, though the obvious answer, still feels like the wrong idea. He checks his watch, wants to be sure to be at the club on time tonight, find an opening to talk to her. Of course she is due for a day off and might not be there tonight. A chilling thought, could wreck his already dismal day, could make *him* groan. What would she do on a night off? Whom would she spend time with? Carroll feels a pang in his tummy; it will not be a good night. Best to concentrate on what can be done. His car is getting too warm, so he sits upright, tries to stay alert for the next breeze. Surely one will come, in this of all places. This guy on the radio—TV, drive-in, glass towers, and all—this guy must have at least *that* much pull.

Go on, he thinks, hope for the best. The thing to do now is to drive home and shower in preparation for his evening. Hell, if he can even get home in time for his evening it'll be a miracle. Adam will never speak—write— to him again, and so what. This week at work he should be able to find time to ship the Corelle Livingware along with a note of apology, which will all be merely a gesture; the apology will be sneered at, and the dishes will be broken in transit. It's not really anything for him to worry about anymore. Adam will get back what he invested. Still, he hopes their marriage goes well. He hopes the new couple is happy, he really does. He'll put that in the note: *I hope the new couple is happy.* Maybe his sincerity will show through and make up for his absence. Maybe the trick is to want good things—not just say it, but actually teach yourself to want it. If he writes that line in the note, meaning it with all his meager might, then isn't that better than showing up, resenting Adam the whole time for getting him lost? It'd be great if little niceties, fond wishes and genuine compliments and such, circled the universe after being launched from a mouth, a pen, or a smile, hung around all of us like a community suit of armor against bad luck and bad intentions, like the huge jar of pennies in his great-grandmother's kitchen. It looked enormous to him. Mom gave him one to add each time they visited, always saying something about a rainy day, and sure enough, the next time he saw it it had more in it. It didn't cost anything to speak of, nobody had to do anything much to make it, but still it grew, and he was led to believe that if called upon it would have the power to shield all of them from any disaster that might befall them. He should have got Adam a jar and a penny instead of Corelle Livingware . . . but that would be too corny. Boy, he thinks, would that be corny.

Got to assume that his luck will hold and that Stevie will be there tonight. If he looks at this any other way he'll collapse. Things will work out fine. This is a small thing, what he did with his hand, and she has a forgiving heart, he just knows she does. People in relationships go through millions of problems. He can talk her through this thing. She must know that he never meant any harm, that he simply didn't know how to behave and got a little carried away. It was, after all, an act of love, that touch. If he can make her see that. An act of love. His hand moved with his heart, that's all. It's not like he hurt her, he wasn't waiting in the parking lot with a knife. He would never ever do anything bad to her. A world of gesture, everything means something, nothing travels alone. At the airport, always more suitcases than people. He'd do anything for her. Heck, Stevie, I'd do nothing for you if that's what you want. I can wait. I can wait and do nothing else. How about it? Waiting, that must count for something, right?

Amidst the annoyed glances of his fellow attendees, Carroll pulls quietly out of the lot. He doesn't want to disturb anyone, but for him these services are over. The radio crackles and gets momentarily louder as he passes through the gate, making one final plea for his attention. "Will Good always flourish in the absence of Evil?" the guy on the radio wants to know. "Or do we find there a spiritual vacuum, a ground to be planted, lifeless soil that we must cultivate until it is a garden of faith to be fostered? Is failing to do Wrong the same as doing Right? And ask yourself, is failing to do Right the same as doing Wrong?"

"Well," says Carroll aloud, alone in his car, "is it?"

But he is on the road outside the cathedral's grounds now, and the radio sputters away into the oblivion of dead air.

It takes him so long to snake his way home through the self-misdirections and traffic backups that have become an integral part of his freeway experience that it's almost ten o'clock by the time he approaches Los Angeles on the 405 and realizes that he's coming up on the exit for Indiscretions and that, though he feels funny about wearing a suit there and looking too much like the regular regulars, it might be prudent to go straight to the club without going home to change first. So he does it, thinking at the last moment to remove his tie and having to walk back across the gravel and unlock the Vega to stash it on the passenger seat. Parking was easy, Sundays being not the busiest night to begin with and ten o'clock on Sunday being less impressive still. He pays at the door, probably just imagining the double take that the DJ/doorman gives him. The guy looks confused, like he knows he's seen Carroll and he knows he's seen guys in suits but he never saw them at the same time before. Well, thinks Carroll, too busy with his own problems to deal with this, so I'm suddenly something new in the world for him. Not that new though, as the bored cocktail waitress, seeing him come in from across the room, looks at the barmaid and says snidely, "Guess you'd better break open another case of that apple stuff, the Lone Ranger is back."

Jasmine is working her way around the stage. Her routine of systematic progression suffers right along with the business of this place, causing her to look like a billiard ball moving in straight lines between spots on opposing cushions. He has his pick of seats tonight and decides to return to the far side of the stage, where he spent most of his nights before Stevie showed up and managed to throw his world into turmoil. But before he can go two steps that new girl from last night pops up right in front of him.

"Hi. My name is Andrea and I'm new here at Indiscretions—"

He lifts his hand to silence her. Somehow this is really insulting, that she wouldn't even remember him from just one night ago. "We met last night," he says, feinting left then right in an attempt to pass her, as if he were demonstrating some lame football play.

She shrugs and turns away murmuring an apology. He thinks he hears the words *of course,* and this transformation of a mistake into a lie rankles him even further. He just wants to sit down and start looking for Stevie, and if he can get there before the end of this set Jasmine will be glad to have the extra stop along the rail. He passes the cocktail waitress, standing at the bar chatting. She seems to smile at him, but when he nods in return a big tall black guy pushes past him and responds to her with a *Heya there,* or something like that. Carroll reddens as they slip their arms around each other and turn to the bar in animated conversation. He doesn't believe it for a second, that those two are buddies, and he loathes how phony this place can be. Here they're all touchy-feely, but if that guy knocked on her door at three in the morning she'd be dialing six different kinds of 911. Around the bulk of the stage and almost home to the side he wants when a man wearing work clothes and a tool belt pops out of the men's room and whacks Carroll's arm with the back of his hand.

"It's all done," he says. "You can go now."

"Huh?" says Carroll, too annoyed to be really curious. It's one fucking little thing after another tonight.

At this Tool Belt looks disgusted himself. "You're not the guy? I mean, you're not the guy. There was a guy out here that wanted to use the head." This isn't enough; the men stare at each other. "I was working on the toilet, fixing it. It's okay now if you want to use it. (almost there) Do you want to use the bathroom?" asks Tool Belt at last.

"No," says Carroll curtly.

But as the conversation closes he realizes that he does, and now he won't be able to for like ten minutes, or at least until the guy leaves or isn't looking. And this is perfect. This fits right in with the day, right in line, right behind every miserable moment that's led him to this point. A whole fucking marching army of miserable moments. He gets to a chair, sits down, and doesn't even bother to get up and look when he senses a puddle on the chair being absorbed into his suit pants. Best case would be a spilled drink—it does feel cold—but he's not about to stand up now and bend over backward to get the bad news. Besides, where would he go to clean it? The men's room?

So who cares, forget it. Watch Jasmine. Tip her. Clear your head and look for Stevie. That bitch of a cocktail waitress knows he's here but is too busy talking with her boyfriend du jour to bring him a cider. Well Fuck Her, and he turns his attention to the stage. Jasmine looks just miserable, and Carroll reflects on how it must be a little humiliating on slow nights like this to have to get naked and act like you care for a fistful of jerks and even fewer dollars. Though he shouldn't and can't afford it, he puts a five-dollar bill on the rail for her. At least it's something, and when she sees it they'll have something between them for the duration of her set. Jasmine dances around, station to station yet abandoning her usual in-line progression and adopting a side-to-side bounce to make the most of the dearth of customers. Carroll awaits his visit; she spotted the five, and it shouldn't be long now. But the song ends without even a pause in front of him. Worse, because he came in in the middle of her set, she has only one song to go. Five bucks is a lot of money for him to spend on a rail tip. Of course he would never take it back, couldn't once she saw it, and he can only hope that she's saving him for the third song. He's seen that before, he'll probably get the whole thing, get looked at nasty by the other men. He looks around during the break: Tina, Nikki, no Stevie yet, probably in the dressing area. He tries to see through the split in the curtain but he can't make anything out from this angle. It is dead, and he has seen them send girls home early on slow nights, and it might be her night off altogether. . . . God, he hopes not! He can't face that after this day, won't be able to stand letting their relationship continue on this sour note for another twenty-four hours.

"One more time for the lovely Jasmine, gentlemen, out in a moment with the third of three," says the DJ/ doorman. That fucker always goes behind the curtain on the side for some reason. He gets to see everything. "Coming up next, lovelylady by the name of . . . lovelylady by the name of Melissa, gentlemen . . . coming up right after Jasmine with the . . . third . . . no . . . yes, the third of three."

Melissa? His heart sinks. He really needed it to be Stevie next, and considering the size of the crowd, the fact that it isn't means it's even more doubtful that she is here at all. Jasmine takes the stage. He knows he'll have to be attentive to her when she comes over, but now that his hopes of seeing Stevie tonight are vanishing, he is in no mood for smiling. Even the door to the ladies' room—he's been eyeing it since he walked in—hasn't opened once. Nobody could be in there that long, not here at this place. Still, perhaps a glimmer of hope? Jasmine looks like she's about to come over, just finishing up with a guy on the other side who has two singles in front of him. Look at him, sitting there looking shamelessly right up at her as if two bucks buys him the world, as if (oh Christ! now he's leaning forward) his two-buck timer is running. Carroll wants to scream at this guy: *Fuck You!* Fuck him! What? does he think that's a five he's got out there? Carroll sits back and folds his arms, ready to enjoy again, though for different reasons, Jasmine's visit. Show that jerk what two bucks'll get him. He knows that she's meticulous about sharing her time equally with each guy on the stage, so five bucks is a strictly gratuitous gesture when Jasmine is dancing. Of course Two Bucks, whom he's never seen here before, wouldn't know that and so looks terribly impressed with his own savvy in buying this extra attention. Finally she is done with him, but she moves next not to Carroll, but to the guy sitting four seats down from him. She was just at this guy . . . what gives?

Stunned, he watches her make the circuit again, pausing once more for each man at the rail except him, not even catching his eye, or letting him catch hers, moving about as if she doesn't see him at all, let alone the fiver before him. This is awful. Unbelievable. Could it be that Stevie warned everybody about him? Does she hate him that much? And where the hell is she? Did she quit because of him? The music for Jasmine's set ends, and she leaves the stage without once dancing in front of him and his five dollars. He sits there fuming, beside himself. He wants to find Stevie, and the most expeditious way to determine if she is working tonight will be to ask someone. But he can't move. He needs to sit where he is and resolve this Jasmine thing first. She'll have to acknowledge him when she comes around to collect her tips. After all, five dollars is normally considered kiss-on-the-cheek material, so she'll have to at least look at him. Waiting, scanning the room as if in search of a witness to this injustice, his eyes fall upon the cocktail waitress, still at the bar. She's looking right at him! There she is with nothing to do. Here he sits with nothing to drink. She knows it, and still she does nothing. Laughing and leaning her elbows on the bar, she looks back to the barmaid and runs a finger around the rim of a glass languidly, to confirm, Carroll knows, that she has no intention of bringing him a drink.

Now it feels like everyone is looking at him, and he suddenly wonders if this is all imagination. Is this what it means to go insane? Once at work he watched Security drag an associate from his office. The guy had barricaded himself inside and wouldn't come out. Everyone thought he was working, but on day two he started screaming and banging the walls. When they finally yanked him out he peered around at the gathering, looking like death incarnate, tight little eyes, beating down hard. Everyone was there, and the guy kept yelling for them to stop staring at him. Cocaine paranoia, they murmured amongst themselves, but they *were* staring.

He suddenly realizes that Jasmine is past him, collecting tips on the end of the stage, and indeed, his five dollars is gone. He has no recollection of her being in front of him. Anger, never before like this in this place, sweeps over his face, and in his fist he balls up one of the discarded cocktail napkins that litter the counter.

"Hey!" he says loudly, brusquely, and it crystallizes the moment. Now everyone really is looking at him. All the conversation, even the music, has been sucked into the vacuum of that word. His move.

He rises unsteadily and moves to the part of the rail that Jasmine is backing away from. In a place like this there are, of course, contingency procedures for such behavior, and he can already feel things begin moving around him. Not from the customers—they all sit motionless like a good audience, like it's the most unobtrusive way to distance themselves from any association with The Problem— but from the corpulent figures with scars on their faces who lurk in the dingy back rooms. Beasts you never see but know are always around a place like this. Carroll's never been in a fight, much less in a place like this.

Carroll is suddenly not so sure he ever belonged in a place like this.

"Hey . . . ," he says again, gripping the rail.

Jasmine holds her ground but is ready to bolt. She checks the bar to confirm that she is safe, though she knows she is. The room is absolutely silent.

"What," she says.

He wishes he knew what he wants to ask her. He really does. At first he thought it was about the tip, but he doesn't care about that now. Then he thought he was going to ask her about Stevie, but he knows that no one here will give him any information like that. Not now. He can feel someone bearing down on him. Turns out it's the black guy who was talking to the cocktail waitress when he walked by. Carroll feels pressure, a strong hand on the back of his neck.

"You gotta leave, man," says the black. The voice is disarmingly civil, if not downright affable, but the hand will clearly remain on Carroll's neck until the night air is felt. "Best you shoulda stayed home tonight."

He allows himself to be led out without any further disruption, laughing inwardly at the understatement: he *should* have stayed home tonight. And he means it. As weak as some of the nights have been, this is the first time he has ever regretted coming to this place. They reach the door. Sure enough, the hand is gone from his neck when they pass to the outside. From there his escort watches him walk alone to and start his Vega. The sheer bulk of this man standing at the door keeps the curious inside where they belong. A small favor to both of them: you and me, we're not monkeys. Carroll backs into a parked car as he is maneuvering out of the lot, but neither he nor the black seems to care about this.

So many lights, here, the village, all up and down Wilshire Boulevard, mark in one way or another so much traffic, people going and coming far below her lofty balcony. It's never too late around here, and the air is warm but not warm enough to chase the tickling chill from a droplet of melting semen as it falls from her vagina and makes its desperate way along her thigh. Stevie lifts her feet to the patio chair and hugs her knees, pulling her short silk robe around her like a cocoon. Inside, snoring on the bed, is her boyfriend, here on one of his increasingly rare visits. No call before the dropping in, and what the hell *did* that mean anyway? All those people. All those problems. Tonight's news ran a story of a newly immigrated Lebanese family, the father, the sole supporter, shot dead on his second week in his new American home, a bystander in a drive-by shooting. Wife was under sedation, but sons and daughter cried for the hungry camera, as if in supplication, cables from the station's remote perhaps extending to heaven. Another drop of semen falls, this time down along the tender fold of her buttock. Men below eat their dinner out of Dumpsters. Boyfriend has already apologized about the sorry state of even this neighborhood and that she has to live with this and he'll see about tighter security. Indeed, somebody down there needs tighter security. But she knows that she'll never be pretty enough or naked enough or fuck good enough to keep those men away from those Dumpsters, and another drop of semen falls from her vagina. No worries there, puddle or no. The worst part of the operation was that it hurt. It seemed like the right thing to do, like it fit, like when she looked at her life it fit. Smoothing out an aberration, and now he can shoot whatever he wants into her with no fear of a costly little heir apparent running up his attorney's fees next year. It did hurt, but she'll be damned if she can feel anything down there now. Just numb. Just cold drops of dead semen and it's just as well because we gotta get some better security to keep those bastards from licking our tossed-out frozen-food packages. Dad took one between the eyes, now do we stay or do we go? A bullet between the eyes wouldn't be all that bad if it kept you from seeing those bastards licking our tossed-out frozen-food packages. At least it would keep them from stinging. She collects on her fingers a smear of his semen, his cast-out come, and rubs it under, into her eyes. They sting. They do sting.

Monday

Solo, the SoLo/Bombgate file, has, evidently, been found. Found, that is, if the scribbled note from Pam, who worked over the weekend, is to be believed. So he dragged himself in here early for nothing. Client's coming in, file's found, problem's over. But that's not the point, not anymore. Call it a piece of good news after the worst day of his life, and let it go. But where was it? He looked everywhere. How could he have not been the one to find it? This was Carroll's project. He terrorized himself looking for that file, and he should have been the one to find it. At this early hour on a Monday the office is still pretty empty, and if Pam worked over the weekend she likely figures that she owes herself an extra half hour of sleep this morning. For that matter what's *he* doing here now? He's the one who should be getting an extra half hour of sleep. But of course, the best it would have been is an extra half hour of staring at his TV—turned off, all night he stared at it turned off. He decides to run down the hall and take a look on her desk.

It wasn't so bad, the not sleeping, with the world so silent like it gets, punctuated by the on-off cycle of his refrigerator so that the offs seem that much quieter when they come around, him lying there, the air so thick with aloneness that he could smell it, taste it on his tongue in the morning in place of the usual pungent coating of residual sleep, which always feels left there like a wafer that was dissolved during the night. Apart from the dead screen of his television, he also watched the meager reflections cast by streetlight through his window take the ceiling with projections of various shapes in the room. They were so faint that you couldn't see them by looking right at them, but the moment you looked away there they were again. It reminded him of the Pleiades, of tenth-grade astronomy class. The teacher had told them to look for the little cluster of stars one evening, warning them that it would only be visible to their peripheral vision. No one bought this, and predictably there were kids the next day who defiantly claimed they had seen the whole schmear looking right at it. Carroll doubted that, he himself had looked for the cluster the night before and the way to do it was to find it, look right at it and see nothing but where it is, then look a tad to one side and see as much as you're permitted to see. Those kids needed to be right—it didn't matter what about—but Carroll knew better. And that's how it was with the lights on his ceiling last night. But as the night wore on he noticed that they were vanishing from even his peripheral vision, and he realized that the sun was moving in on them. Again, not yet strong enough that you could notice any brightening of the room or sky, but you just sensed the change on some primal level long ago dismissed by the species, as if someone you trusted implicitly called you up and told you that the sun was rising, and though you couldn't see it at all you believed that person. You believed it so much that pretty soon you started to imagine it was getting lighter. Carroll figured a solid hour had passed between the time he imagined it getting lighter and the moment his eyes told him it really was getting lighter. Actual sunrise, he knew from watching the Almanac segment of the Weather segment of the News on TV last week, was still a long way off.

So it wasn't so bad, lying there awake. Nothing like the drive home. Now that was bad. He passed the airport, drove under that huge runway bridge just as a jet was taxiing across it. Until then he had been driving in a sort of pleasant daze, like, he supposes, maybe drunks drive, though he didn't weave. And he remembers everything. Hitting that car in the parking lot and not stopping to leave a note (even if he had thought to do it it hardly would have been appropriate). When he felt the impact Carroll looked instinctively to the door of the club and saw the black guy who had walked him out standing there alone. Carroll smiled like they were old friends, but later realized that there was no way for the guy to notice this from across the lot in the dark. He did let him pull away though, so he must not have been too concerned about the car Carroll hit. And Carroll kept that silly smile on his face as he drove down Imperial Highway, banking right with the easy curve of a traffic triangle onto Sepulveda. Everything was fine, like a queer out-of-his-hands relief had washed over him. Not thinking, just smiling. He drove north on Sepulveda, heading toward the little green VENTILATION OK light that guards the entrance of the runway tunnel and feeling okay himself. But he shouldn't have felt okay, and as if to correct this flaw in the glass a huge TWA 747 suddenly consumed the sky and the runway above him just as he rolled into the tunnel. Now this may not sound like much, but even on a mundane day you can count on a fast education about the enormity of Man's machines down at the airport when car meets jet meeting bridge, and for Carroll, whose day had been anything but mundane, the experience had less to do with Man's machines than it did with a veritable wake-up call from the darkest places of his mind. Big fire-fucking angel from hell steps into the picture right when it's too late for him to do anything but crawl under its belly and hope for the best. So ended the pleasant daze, and the rest of the drive home was riddled with anxiety and terror, regret and despair.

The jet of course had served its purpose and wasn't to be found anywhere in his rearview mirror, though he kept looking there, as he emerged from the tunnel and proceeded along Sepulveda, past the airport, the billboards that sing specious songs of lavish accommodations to the ears of expense-account–endowed travelers. Carroll inched upward to get a look at himself in his mirror and found there a face as white as the balled-up cocktail napkin, which he then discovered in his hand. He wiped his brow, causing his hand to start shaking, and returned to the road before him while continually checking the mirror to confirm what lay behind him. Something very bad was in that mirror; he caught glimpses of it behind the eyes he met there. It shone in a flash deep within the nether reaches of his pupils, shone with an intensity that fairly lit up the car so brightly and quickly that when he looked again it lived only in the photosensitive memory of the luminous dials that dot his dashboard. The closure, he couldn't ignore it: never again may he return to Indiscretions. Headlights of the opposing traffic, when the cars came upon him, locked onto his gaze and stung his eyes the way a welding torch high above and across the street can still manage to stab through the daylight and cause you to wince. The devastating truth of how this terminus would affect his life grew perniciously in his belly. Never again . . . never, never, never again see Stevie. Never park in the lot, never walk through the door, never see the inside of That Place, never see Melissa, Tina, Nikki, anyone. Never again do what lies at the center of his world. He had to slam on the brakes to make the turn onto Santa Monica Boulevard, and the jerk of his body in the seat was all that was needed to manage the trick. He choked, and before he could stop himself, vomited on the steering wheel and his lap. Not much, but messy, caught some on his arms when he had to steer through it. Between him and his apartment was a long stretch of stoplights, even heavy traffic in West Hollywood in the middle of the night. And once he got there, once he got home, what could he do? Clean up? Wait for work?

You can always tell when someone works over the weekend by the way their desk is all straightened up Monday morning. No one would dare waste time doing that during regular hours. It'd be like begging for overflow work from someone less fortunate whose desk appropriately reflects their overwhelming workload. Pam's desk looks sharp, and Carroll bets that if keeping it that way weren't a breach of office etiquette it always would. He likes Pam. He'd like to see her tell her boss to fuck off one day. But she'll never say that. No, that would never happen. Maybe that's why he likes her.

With the desk clean like this it doesn't take long for him to find the file. He doesn't even have to look in the drawer. It's sitting squarely in the center of her desk pad, presumably in anticipation of today's meeting with the client. Nor does it take long for him to realize that this isn't really the file at all. Just by picking it up he can feel that it's merely the jacket to the SoLo/Bombgate file, an expandable sleeve made out of sturdy red cardboard and cloth. Called a RedWeld by the vendor from whom they're ordered, they cost a fortune, something like $4.65 apiece. He makes these things up for newly opened files every day by punching some holes and adding some labels. He made this one up back when the file was opened, remembers thinking that it was some sort of milestone when he typed the assigned number: So-Lotions Inc. vs. Morris Bombgate 089000–090. But even a new jacket has folders and clips in it, places to organize the various correspondence, documents, and pleadings. This is just an empty jacket. Useless. He can only assume that Pam put the contents on her boss's desk—she had specifically mentioned the documents and litigation clips when they were still looking for it. That doesn't explain where the rest of it is, or why it would be separated to begin with. But she wouldn't have called off the search if she didn't have that stuff, and if it's found, it's found. He's tempted to take a look in her boss's office, but he couldn't face anymore drama right now. He'll wait and ask her when she gets in.

He can't help but feel, walking away from Pam's desk, a sense of loss at the file's having been found, a deadness at having these events pass him by, and this in the wake of the horror he engendered last night, when he alone led those events way beyond anyplace they should have gone. There must be something in between, a way to move without falling down, a way to feel without pinching yourself. This is silly; there's no reason in the world he can't walk in and see if those clips are in Pam's boss's office. He turns around and retraces his steps to her secretarial bay. Around the corner and down the hall the bell of an arriving elevator sparkles: *I'm Here!* The morning is in motion, and people are plodding in to seize the day.

Not receiving an answer to his tentative knock on Pam's boss's door, Carroll gingerly slips into the darkened office. Drapes drawn, you don't often see that. The desk looks okay, but he knows better, knows that this is one of those guys who craves neatness without necessarily requiring order. Sure, the papers are stacked, but the stacks don't represent any classification beyond a uniform size. The file fragments he is seeking are not readily visible, so he begins examining these stacks of paper. Fortunately most of them have ridiculous paperweights on them, which when lifted betray an accumulation of dust by revealing a dustless area in the shape of their little Lucite or mahogany bases. Here are two kids frozen under glass: *World's Greatest Pop!* they claim. Nothing there. He checks under what looks like a big brass strawberry . . . no, it's a nut: *Buckeye–Barnes Association/Honors/1979/Cleveland Plaza Hotel.* Nope. Next he lifts a Lucite cube with a miniature book sealed inside but doesn't bother to read whatever corporate mumbo-jumbo is written on the tiny cover. Uh-uh. How about this one, a model car, a red Lotus, little doors open and everything, he used to play with these as a kid, had a whole collection. SoLo/Huntley, dash 093, close but no cigar. Still, the car's kind of neat, and he wonders if this guy drives a Lotus. Not with those kids, he thinks, looking back to the hunk of glass, they look demanding. He checks a few more stacks, some improbable loose papers, and finally the credenza, which sees little use in this office due to the fact that it is laden with antique law books. Like this is gonna impress a client: *Well sure, it might be illegal now, but what about back in aught-six? Could I have done it then?* Zippo. There's not one fucking SoLo/Bombgate document in this office. Nothing. The harder you look the less you find. Applies to everything, all around, fucked. He leaves the office, lost in thought as he pulls slowly the door behind him. This guy, Pam's boss, that's a life in there. All that stuff, or at least some of it, is important to him. All in all it's nothing to laugh at. He suddenly feels soft for this guy, and he wonders what would happen if he ever tried to shake his hand, or pat him on the back affectionately. But that would never fly; might as well try to kiss him on the cheek. It takes both caution and serendipity to make friends in this world, and even then the ones you cling to don't want to hear about it. This guy, Pam's boss, he's got his own questions. Nothing to laugh at now, especially now.

Okay. So what? Maybe Pam took the individual clips home to work on them. But then why not take the jacket?

No, it doesn't make sense. No way around it, he'll just have to wait for her to come in so he can talk to her. He pulls shut the office door, which clicks now at his flank.

"Carroll?" says Pam circumspectly, startling him and casting about for a reason to be suspicious. Looking ready for battle in her trenchcoat and armed with purse, lunch, and satchel, she just now came upon him as he stood outside her boss's door. Well no crime in that, she supposes. "You're here bright and early," she allows as she yields her face to a friendlier fold.

He's unsure of how much she saw, unsure if he cares. "Pam. Hi. I got your note. I guess I wanted to take a look at the file after spending so much time looking for it." He gestures ambiguously, encompassing the whole area with his arms but settles on, "So I looked on your desk, but all that's there is the jacket. Did you take the file home? Maybe it's in his office?" (a shouldered thumb, denial of hindsight).

"Just the jacket?" asks Pam, glancing at her desk for reassurance and evidently finding it. "What do you mean? The file's right there." She sets down her lunch and lifts the red cardboard jacket: here.

Could she not know that it's empty? "That's what I mean," he says, moving toward and taking it from her. "It's empty. See. (he shakes it upside down) This is just the jacket. The file itself is gone." She still looks nonplussed, so he adds, "Maybe your boss has it. Maybe he came in over the weekend after you left and took out the clips."

She drops the rest of her stuff as well as her shoulders, unloading her burden with all the vexation of a furniture mover being victimized by an indecisive housewife. "That's the file, Carroll. That's what I found. Sure, maybe there's a clip or two scattered around with some of the guys, but that's the file. That's it!" Taking it out of his hand and shaking it for herself, though this time right side up: "This is it!"

Getting hot. His face is getting hot. "But that's *not* it. That's only the jacket. Pam, you said yourself that you needed some original documents from the file . . . and what about the litigation clip? Didn't you say you wanted that? This is just the jacket! This is nothing. If this was all you wanted I could have made up a new one in two minutes. What good is this gonna do? You said the client was coming in and they needed the file today. Are you gonna hand him this? Is this gonna make him happy?" So much emotion, a lifetime of it packed into a couple of hours, it seems like. He feels out of control but different from last night. He feels right, feels like he shouldn't walk away, shouldn't even move his feet. This is broken outside, this is not broken inside.

She senses him flying out of control, and she has a maternal urge to temper him. But she also thinks enough is enough, and isn't her day going to be bad enough without playing nursemaid to a file clerk? "Carroll, Carroll, listen. I simply said that there were original docs with the file. We don't need them today, and they'll turn up as soon as whoever is working with them is finished. Last week I typed up a new motion to dismiss. That's all the litigation clip that the client will need to see." He looks the same to her, looks like he'll be standing there for a thousand years. Well, enough is enough. After all, if he were a genius he wouldn't still be in the file room. "I don't expect you to understand. This client likes to come in and sign papers and have lunch, okay? He'll be plenty happy to see this file sitting on the desk. It's fine. This action is ancient, and what does he know from files anyway? He'll be thrilled." She busies herself for effect, ostensibly positioning her satchel and purse in their respective places. "You did a fine job for us—you know I always count on you—but this is over. Now Carroll, I've got a lot of work today. (he doesn't get the hint) I need you to leave me alone so I can get to it. (doesn't move) Leave, Carroll!" she says, clearly angry, and commences ignoring him.

He bites his lower lip, casts about the hall for an answer. "He'll be happy with that?" he demands.

But Pam says nothing, just nods her head once, almost imperceptibly. He turns and walks down the hall. His own choice, looking for a lost file that everyone else thinks is found, and in this office there won't be a lot of sympathy for his plight. One thing matters here: billing hours. No, here he is very much alone.

The desk doesn't seem a possibility, not his, not once he gets a look at it from the doorway of the file room, looking as he is through those red eyes, those red eyes that everyone gets and that grow more and more deleterious with each passing year until a guy finds himself calculating the ratios of shots per second and fast-food customers per square yard, and while Carroll isn't about to go that route, neither is he ready to go back to his desk and sit there typing file inventories like a good little cookie. Still, he doesn't want another scene like last night, at least not without thinking it through. Maybe a walk—he turns right around and heads back toward the elevators— maybe a walk . . .

. . . into the West Los Angeles morning, and in this part of town that makes him the only pedestrian in sight.

Okay, so there are a few people here and there running
between buildings, but he is certainly the only one around
who is taking a Walk. Not necessarily a safe bet; the cars
out here on Olympic Boulevard are piloted by people who
would be hard pressed to define the word *pedestrian*, wan-
ton professionals with shouldered car phones and opened
briefcases who would look upon the charge of Vehicular
Homicide as mostly a pain in the appointment grid before
they discovered with dismay that it can't be wiped off
their record by electing an evening at comedy traffic
school. Nevertheless Carroll crosses against the light, causing brakes to be reluctantly applied. There's a 7–Eleven
down the block, and though he's never been to this one,
it now draws him like a magnet. A big, chalky, red and
green magnet, he thinks, whatever the hell that means. His
concern for the whereabouts of the Solo file—or rather, its
contents—has waned, been supplanted by frustration and
nagging questions, questions about how these people
could turf so readily on this. It's like they couldn't wait to
gobble up not The Solution but any solution, or like the
first solution, by virtue of its being available, became for
them The Solution. Sounds like a great way to make it to
the morning coffee break, but what's left to come back to
when the decaf is drunk and the Twinkies eaten? And as
if all that weren't bad enough, he finds, as he walks along
busy Olympic Boulevard, that he can't help trying to look
at the people in the cars, especially the blonds. If he catches
a flash of blond go by at fifty-two mph he tracks it like a
spectator at an auto race. Sometimes he's wrong and there
is no blond. But other times he doesn't notice the blond
until his head is already in motion. Amazing. More magnets. Of course he knows he isn't going to find her like this,

driving by in a car. That would be a long shot even if he knew where she lived and staked out her street, much less standing here in the middle of the morning commute. A woman like Stevie you wouldn't see by accident, because if you *did* see her, then it wouldn't be an accident.

The 7-Eleven is doing a brisk business, what with forty-ounce javas, cellophane-wrapped breakfast goodies, and a microwave on the premises. The clientele is surprisingly blue collar, not at all in keeping with the look of the drive-by traffic. But this doesn't save Carroll from the derisive looks dealt to anyone shady enough to be *walking* up to a place like this. They know something must be wrong, and to play it safe they give him a little sneer, better yet a murmur capped with snickers, a little special bonding with a friend in the passenger seat. Carroll runs the gauntlet of freelance cable installers and beat pickups laden with lawn mowers and Mexicans. Once inside the door he looks to his left and notices the familiar color-coded height sticker running up the doorframe. Impossible to tell how tall you are by one of these things, he'd probably have to rob the store, pause here on his way out the door, and wait for his public defender to get a hold of the witness report before he could get his own height. A long way to go for an official stat. Still, it's nice to be noticed. He takes a few steps around the congested aisles, wondering if there isn't something to eat that might calm him down but knowing that even if there is he isn't likely to find it in this place. For the other customers, who know exactly where to look for what they get every day, he is very much underfoot, and they impatiently push past him, just as they would speed around a disoriented driver who slows to read addresses on a busy street. Looks of exasperation and superiority crowding their faces, they home in on the goody in question, perhaps a Breakfast Sausage Bun-Yum or an Oat Bran Berry-Bagel, snatch it from the shelf or bin with dispatch, and fall into line at the register, only to secretly agonize about whether to go back and get one that isn't squished on the side, and fuck that idiot who stood over my shoulder and made me hurry when I picked this one out. Carroll tries the candy section, sees nothing he wants. Slurpees, soft-serve ice cream, cereal, dental floss, brownies, Brillo pads, soup, nuts, he looks in the dairy case, sees the milk then walks all the way around the store to the honey. There is nothing here he can use, nothing that will help him this morning. He shuffles out to the parking lot, leaving the busy clerks less worried about what he may have boosted than about what manner of corporate Big Brotherism may have caught them looking less worried. Outside on Olympic Boulevard a passing semi barreling through a yellow light raises the dust of the street to a swirling cloud that moves to settle about the 7-Eleven lot. Motley litter takes a short old ride. It's like this all over.

With no idea what to do, except not to go back to work yet, he continues walking east. Heavy traffic pounds his back with the vacuum of speed, sucking him along the periphery as if entreating him to get with the program and buy a car, rent one, even hop a bus, anything! In truth they want more; any car won't do. His Vega, when he's in it, is always subject to contempt from the other drivers. They look right through him on the road, look surprised when, after speeding like hell to reach his rear bumper, they suddenly realize that they can't drive over him. Los Angeles is not exactly a safe haven for American cars built in the seventies. Where do they all go? In the East they stay on the road forever, even with the rust. Perhaps one night the Vega will be seized, taken out of his apartment garage under cover of darkness, wrapped in blankets and spirited away to a clandestine debriefing center in the desert. Rebuilt and repainted, it will surface months later at a snow-covered car lot in Cleveland, Ohio, dazed, headlights vacuous as they stare out from under the words E-Z TERMS! Carroll stumbles, looks down, and realizes that, halfway along this sunny block, the sidewalk has degenerated into a mostly dust path. Like a sidewalk ruin, there is a bit of man-made surface every five or six feet along the path, skew pieces that seem to be pushing up from under the dust and gasping for air, or maybe they're still sinking. Hard to tell. Might be merely different parts of the same process.

This section of LA is zoned in such a way that tall commercial structures tower over residential blocks. This can't have been going on all that long, for the commercial buildings are not that old and the houses look mostly paid-off. In some places remnants of an old neighborhood business district can still be discerned between the granite and glass and the well-kept lawns, very much so at the intersection on which he now stands, up the cross street and past the next light. Here lies a small storefront bar under a busted neon sign, busted neon in the shape of a farm animal, busted in such a manner that there's no way to further identify the animal, farm in fact being indicated only by the faded straw painted near its . . . hooves? No matter, anyone sitting in this place has likely been sitting there long enough to learn, know, and forget the name.

Except Carroll, who impulsively drops out of his walk and bumps through the door.

Even darker than Indiscretions, is his first thought, and the name rekindles a pang that now feels like it will be ever near, ever clear, in his own dark places. It's awfully early for a bar to be open, let alone have customers, drinking customers, though one guy does seem to be having coffee. But Carroll knows that there are people who drink at this hour, drink, in fact, around the clock. His own experience with alcohol is limited to a sip of champagne (which he never would have touched except the office manager put it in his hand and practically made it sound like drinking it was part of his job description) at his first and only Christmas party at the firm. It tasted funny, and he had no way of knowing if it was spoiled (it was sort of warm) or if all champagne tasted that way. So he poured it down the sink when no one was looking. Then he drank some Tab and left, never going to another office party, always pleading a previous commitment, which was true: shortly after that was when he started frequenting Indiscretions (ouch). So whatever's in it, this drinking business, it's beyond him. On the other hand, he doesn't feel like there's much to lose this morning, and maybe it would be a good time to find out.

As his eyes adjust to the mostly red light in the place he picks out a stretch of three stools and climbs aboard the center one, glad, having now gotten a better look at the other customers, for the buffer zone on either side.

"Yeah!" barks the bartender as he rises from his perch near the well. He seems friendly enough, mostly all business.

Looking down at the square cocktail napkin sliding
to rest on the bar in front of him, Carroll realizes that he
is ill equipped to respond. He knows from watching TV
that this scene works like a script. He's supposed to get
what he always gets, but it doesn't look like sparkling
apple cider will fly here; besides, that's not what he
walked in for.

"What do people usually get?" he tries.

The bartender, old, big, and tough but tempered by
an air of being ready to accept you on his side, sighs, but
he is also amused. He knows that The Guys are now looking on—indeed, the other customers have all looked up
and quieted down their murmurs to listen—and that he
has an obligation to draw out the scene. He can also tell
that this guy is shaken about something and that's why
he's in here, not by any means a drunk.

"Well that depends on if you're a man who drinks
liquor in the morning. Now I also got coffee. Or I could
pour you some juice—orange or grapefruit or cranberry.
Or you could have a beer. Lots of people like a beer to get
started." Both Ors are accompanied by a turned-up palm
and a nod to something under the bar, presumably the
cooler, but the message is clear: this list will be recited only
once. He steals a quick glance at The Guys and lips are
bitten.

Carroll, much to his own surprise, is not terrified.
"Um . . . say, like a rum and Coke. Do people ever get
that?" Then he adds, totally out of the blue, an assertive
tone to his voice when he says, "It's like this: I don't drink,
but I want to now."

At this The Boys begin to lose interest. Carroll just
lost any effeminate quality that they may have detected

in him, and so as sport he is likely to be a disappointment. He's just a funny stiff who doesn't drink, and to them that's just not that funny.

Bartender too knows the game is over, so he plays it straight. Professional, these guys, usually, the best ones are. "You can have that if you want. But if it was me I'd get either a screwdriver or a greyhound. That's juice with vodka. Or if I really wanted to drink serious I'd get a shot or two of whiskey. Have it on ice if you'd rather. Maybe a little water." That oughtta do it.

Carroll's turn. It's one of those times to make your best guess, using the information at hand. "Whiskey then, I guess, with some ice . . . and some water."

Bartender nods and has it to him in no time. "Two bucks," he says, and when Carroll hands him three he adds, "Next one's on me."

Carroll looks at the amber contents of the glass before him, looks to his right and left at the room around him. This may not be the most cheerful place he's ever seen, yet at the same time it doesn't have that menacing undercurrent you always notice in bars in TV movies or cop shows like *Hunter*. While he knows he's being monitored by the men around him, he's pretty sure that everyone here just wants to be left alone. Maybe it's the early hour, but he should be okay as long as he keeps to himself. It sure doesn't smell too good; that you never get from TV. But that's nothing compared to the whiskey in his glass, which is positively noxious.

A guy down the bar is smiling at him. Interested and wanting to be helpful, he suggests, "Best all at once," and by way of demonstration lifts his glass of beer and downs it.

Picking up the whiskey, Carroll apes him, this in total disregard for every signal his body can get out every step of the way, importunately: no, no, no! Of course the next signal is: Puke! Right Now! Just Puke! He gags instead and keeps it down. Slowly and deliberately he rises, thanking the bartender and turning toward the door.

"How 'bout that, eh?" the guy down the bar wants to know.

But Carroll chooses not to respond. Instead he walks outside and into the alley next door, which leads him to a grease and soot encrusted Dumpster at the rear of the building. Here, in relative seclusion, he jams his finger down his throat and gets an immediate reaction. Squatting, to kneeling, to sitting on a plastic dairy crate, he wipes his mouth with his sleeve. This isn't working either. If I focused my life on one thing, talking to Stevie just one more time, that would have to work, right? Right.

Well, that's enough of that, he thinks, sitting at his desk now for the last three hours, ostensibly updating file inventories but in truth biding his time until the Solo client arrives for that afternoon meeting with Pam's boss. Liquorwise he's pretty much recovered, and to cap things off he surreptitiously (though he's alone in the room) takes the final pull from a Pepto-Bismol bottle purchased at a liquor store on the walk back this morning and kept at the ready since then in his bottom drawer. File inventories, he's never seen a single one that wasn't dotted with tiny red stickers used to denote a missing jacket. That's how they always referred to a lost file when he was being trained, a "missing jacket." How would they classify SoLo/Bombgate, the office manager and Sandra, the old clerk? He can hear it now: *Don't stick your neck out.* If they're happy then we're happy. Remember, it's not the finding, it's being able to say it's found, and that's one less red dot on your inventory. Sandra would've said something like that, and the OM would've smiled scandalously: now Sandra . . . , tacitly going along with this dubious procedure while at the same time reserving a lifeboat of disapproval should such an inventory not sail when it finally got upstairs. Carroll stands up from his desk, knocking it and causing the roll of red stickers to fall onto the floor, where it spins a moment before settling goofily, like one of those plastic Slinkys they make nowadays that are supposed to be safer for the kids than the old metal ones but we all know they're just cheaper in plastic. These guys act like saints but it's all in the wallet, or if it is about safety then it's done at the behest of their insurance company's lawyer. That's the real motivation for sainthood these days: fear of litigation. He marches out of the room. Banks of fluorescents burn coolly, hot on his heels.

Pam won't look up (still mad) though she knows he's coming down the hall. Maybe he'll just walk by and annoy someone else with some new crusade.

"So how'd the client like that file, Pam?" he fairly shouts, or at least the loud and clear voice sounds like shouting when one considers the source . . .

. . . sure, he's a nice guy and all that, thinks Pam, but this is not a take-charge dude, say a Gene Hackman in *The Poseidon Adventure* or a Paul Newman in *The Towering Inferno*. Give me an earthquake and you won't find me hightailing it down to the file room for protection. "Are you okay, Carroll?" she asks, like this is the real issue. Then remembering his question: "They're still in there (nod to her boss's door). I told you not to worry about it, it'll be fine."

New computer installations around the office have required alterations to some of the secretarial bays. One of these is next to Pam. Wallpaper is stripped away, drywall cut. The piece Carroll is looking at has Magic Marker on it from one of the workmen; it says, NO CUT HERE. And that's it. So does that mean that you can cut anywhere else, or do you have to look for a marker that says CUT HERE? Maybe it means that they checked and discovered that there exists no cut there, but they're not sure about everywhere else. You don't know. You gotta be that guy, the one who wrote it, or at least you gotta work for him. Otherwise you're on your own. A dry wall indeed, that with the writing on it. Carroll winks at Pam. He can't remember ever winking at anyone before in his life, didn't even know he was able. Some people can't, independent movement evolved right out of their brows, plucked away like the hairs that will surely follow. He turns, raps twice loudly on Pam's boss's door, and throws it open.

No one speaks at first, all waiting for Carroll. The three men in this room look up expectantly, at the ready to get the dope on whatever emergency would require such an improbable intrusion. A nice surprise here is the presence of the fat-fuck corporate partner from twelve, who no doubt just dropped in to say hi. Sitting before the desk in one of the client chairs, he has his hands folded over his crotch and his eyebrow raised, as if about to declare himself the ranking authority in the room and order Carroll shot. Pam's boss, behind the desk, is caught with his arm outstretched in a gesture. He made the unfortunate choice of freezing it when Carroll burst in, and now he's uncertain of how to bring it down (to just do it would be to actually acknowledge this impossible interruption).

The Solo client, in the remaining client chair, can tell that something's up but has no idea what it could be, and he looks back and forth between the two other men for a clue. But to no avail, for it is him whom Carroll addresses, when presently he speaks.

"I'm sorry we were unable to locate the contents of your Bombgate file, sir. But don't worry, it'll turn up, I'll keep—"

"What is this?" demands Pam's boss petulantly. Putting his outstretched arm to good use, he waves Carroll aside, as if to make room for Pam, whom he sees pushing inward from the hall. "Pam! Who is this?"

Meanwhile, the corporate partner manages a stunned, "You!" but it gets lost in the more urgent demands of Pam's boss, who, like it or not, seems to have assumed control here (well . . . it is *his* office).

Solo Client is baffled. The kid is talking to him, but better let these two handle it. Wonder who the hell he is? Probably just some poor drunk underpaid grunt. Awkward. Just wait it out. Hell, Client remembers his own mailroom job. Used to get all the pussy he wanted in that job. Wonder if it's the same these days (though this guy doesn't look up to it). And what the hell is Bombgate? Thought that old thing was dead. Wonder if I'm still being billed for it? Better have Gail check on that.

"Carroll!" Pam entreats, grabbing his arm and tugging.

He looks at the three men before him. Pam's boss is on the verge of rising, for no apparent reason other than to maintain his momentum as the one who will handle this problem. But Carroll can see that he just wants Pam to deal with this, get it out of his life, the way she would a typo in a document or a bond salesman on the phone. Fat Fuck is trying to piece together in his head some witticism with which he hopes to take the client's mind off of the interruption. Don't bother, Carroll wants to tell him, for the client is clearly not concerned with these events, is lost in thoughts of his own while he waits for Carroll to move out of his way like an old lady in a crosswalk. It's obvious (how could he not know it would be like this) that none of these three men cares about anything he has to say. In fact, Solo Client appeared to not even understand the reference to Bombgate, just looked dumb and embarrassed, as if at a dinner party and the hostess's three-year-old just peed in his lap. Even now his eyes wander. Carroll couldn't get his attention if he were sleeping with the guy's daughter, waving her panties around with a broomstick. Maybe he should try reminding him that he's being billed for the time spent on this. That might do it, riveting stuff.

Pam's boss has an inspiration; it's there in his eyes. "Look . . . Carl, we appreciate your concern, but we have all the files we require. Perhaps you should go work this out with Pam and the office manager and (a patiently indulgent smile, forced hard and maybe to his credit) let us get on with our meeting here."

Carroll feels utterly dejected. He allows Pam to pull him from the doorway but breaks away from her in the hall, where he walks evenly to his desk as she goes directly for the phone. He can feel the phone lines buzzing all around him, odious little wires, myriad threads, all mottled and crooked, a big net waiting to be drawn up. He stops and leans against the wall, hitting it with his elbow and causing a startled temp to tap the stop pedal of her Dictaphone. Those things are antiques now, but then there's carbon paper in the supply room as well. That

net, first Pam to office manager, but by now there have
been other calls, OM to Pam's boss, Pam to her friend on
twelve. It gets tighter faster, finally so fast that you're
stuck. On second thought, there's nothing he needs at his
desk, and he could do without the collateral confrontation
with the office manager, who will certainly be heading
there by now to intercept him. Best the elevator. Best commence straightaway with the erasure of this place from his
future. That net. Phones are ringing around him. Paranoia,
sure, but still. . . . You go to all this trouble to cut a hole,
you'd better walk through.

The Vega sputters and almost stalls when he pulls into the
gravel lot, and Carroll wonders again whether this is such
a great idea. But car and driver both regain their resolve
as he crosses into the alley and parks in a place that
allows a good view of the back door to the club as well as
of the lot, most of it. No commitment here, if things go
south he can just pull away.

   Though this wasn't his destination upon leaving for
the last time the parking garage of his office he's not all
that surprised to find himself sitting here. After all, he
wasn't about to go home and this is the only other place
he ever goes. That of course must stop, did stop. He can't
walk into the club; he knows that. But maybe just this one
last time he can sit in the lot. Turns out it's late enough
for the staggered shift change to begin, and with any luck
at all he'll be able to get one final look at Stevie when she
enters the club. He may not know what she drives, and
he can't be absolutely sure she's even working tonight; but
he does know that all the dancers enter through the back
door, and since she was off last night it's likely she'll be

here tonight. But it's okay either way; it's nice just to sit here and look at everyone walk in and out. Relaxing, like maybe how it is to be dead, just sitting at the sidelines, watching others take their turns. The office, now there's a place he is glad to be done with. No, it's not likely he'll be sitting across Olympic Boulevard looking at *that* building with longing eyes anytime soon. Not that he minds working—he's not lazy—but time comes for everyone to make choices, even him, and walking out like that makes twice today that he made himself be sick.

Here comes a black Datsun Z. That'd be Candy; he knows, he saw her get into that car one night last month. Purely by chance, that he saw her, he wasn't spying or anything, just happened to be leaving when she was. She even said goodnight to some guy getting into a car next to her, some customer whom Carroll recognized as a semi-regular. It was pretty perfunctory, like *Goodnight, whoever the fuck you are*, or *Goodnight, come one step closer and I'll scream*, but still it would've been nice if she'd said it to him too. He even fumbled with his keys for a second to give her a chance, even thought she looked his way, but nothing. Into the black Z and gone. then to add insult to injury the guy whom she did speak to looked at him and smiled, gloating like. So Carroll said goodnight to him, but he didn't respond, and later Carroll felt stupid, like the time they were showing off scars in the lunchroom and by the time he got up the nerve to display a childhood cut on his elbow everyone was on to a new topic and ignored him. There he was, sleeve rolled up and no one looking. So he went to the sink and washed his hands as a sort of cover. He was right; that is Candy. Locks her door, into the club and gone.

Two men whom he has seen many times inside just came outside. They walk to their Lincoln and get in the front seat, where, as nearly as he can make out, they take turns pulling on a bottle of something. Probably liquor. The club serves no alcohol by law, Carroll knows, but that doesn't keep the hot shots from drinking. Twice he's walked in on somebody sipping from a small bottle in the men's room, and once he saw a guy adding to his drink below the counter level from a flask he kept in his boot. Now these two guys are getting back out of the Lincoln and returning to the front door. It's supposed to be no in-and-out privileges, like the parking garage at work if you don't have a card, but some guys get in and out all they want. Must be the same guys whose names are on that clipboard kept by the DJ/doorman. Do the drunks and crooks in this world get everything, or do the guys who have everything become drunks and crooks? For his part Carroll would be happy just to talk to Stevie one more time, but that, even if he sees her in the lot, would be risky. She may not have been working last night but you can't tell what she might have heard, can't tell about what friends she has here, what the net at Indiscretions is like. That's getting to be a real liability for him, a mini-crook in his own right. He doesn't want another escort by that black guy, doesn't want to ruin that relationship too, such as it is.

Here comes a white Toyota. But it doesn't park, merely cruises the lot, passing by the empty spaces as well as the taken ones. That sort of thing makes Carroll nervous, but the car swings out into the alley and away without spotting him at all, not that he has any reason to think they would care. A silver something—he can't identify it—pulls into one of the empty spaces after turning fast (practically on two wheels) into the lot. But once the dust settles he can see that it's nothing, just three guys in short-sleeve white shirts and ties, probably done with work for the day, heading for the entrance. That rankles, when you think about it, that these nobodies can waltz in there like they own the place when he has to sit in his car and watch, afraid even to be in the lot. Well, you make your bed. . . . There's that white Toyota again. This time it stops right in the middle of the lot and (surprise) out pops the new redhead from the passenger side. She slams the door and storms into the club. Mad. Must've been a fight because whoever is driving the car speeds away so fast that Carroll can see the gravel kicked up, hitting some of the parked cars, and it takes forever for the dust in the lot to settle.

Here comes a red Ferrari—that's a car you can tell what it is—and he remembers seeing it before, parked in the lot a few times this last week when he was coming and going. It'll be interesting to see which jerk drives a car like that. But as it turns into a space near the back door Carroll sees in a flash of blond hair that the driver isn't a jerk; it's a woman. Wait . . . it isn't just a woman; it's *Her*. Well he shouldn't be surprised. Maybe he even knew it a second before he saw it. It's not important. What matters now is, what does he do?

Not much of a question, that, as Stevie rises out of the car and into his focus. This chick's a magnet, and there's nothing holding him back. He jumps out of the Vega, slamming the door behind him, a smack shot across the lot like a bullet, which makes her start but not look up. Small threat, whatever it is, with the back door of the club so nearby and what the hell. For her, you could say, anything goes. And Carroll is over that gravel before her key leaves the Ferrari door.

"Hi," he ventures carefully, standing offishly, say seven feet from her rear bumper.

Now this does make her jump, and the fact is it's what her boyfriend would call an unacceptable situation. Best plan here would be to call for one of the guys inside, just scream a name (one thing you get here is response time). On the other hand she recognizes Carroll, and while that should be even more cause for alarm in this line of work, she figures a scream is a scream, and maybe she owes this poor guy a . . . moment (and man, she almost thought *a shot at redemption,* and that's one motherfuckin' icy way of thinking there).

"Oh, hi," she says and she shivers. "You startled me. . . . It's Carroll, right? (on his eager nod: use it) You startled me, Carroll." No one around. "We're kind of pushing the rules out here. Why don't we talk inside? I imagine you're going in?"

Netless, I presume. She doesn't know. "I can't," he says, and not without some remorse.

Which remorse she does not fail to detect. This may be an interesting story after all. She grins, accepting, quick nods, like: okay, let's go ahead and talk for a second. Remember, a scream away (silly). "Oh, so you're just leaving. Sorry I missed you. Are you sure you don't want to stay for a while?" Sometimes she feels like a whore. Is she? (Not that again.)

"I (looking down, shuffling of feet) sort of made a scene last night. I had a bad day, and I lost my temper about something stupid, and they asked me to leave." He looks up; she's still there and that's encouraging. "I don't think I'd be very welcome in there now."

Boy, this could be good, though it looks like she'll have to wait. As much as she's beginning to loathe this place, she's now anxious to go inside and get the whole story from one of the other girls. This stuff gets bandied about for days. Still, she can't believe he would've been violent, and really, the best she can do right now is to stay and talk with him for a minute. For sure, it would give him more than it would cost her. "Oh," she says simply, solemnly, making gravity for his sake. Make sure you stick with their up-down thing.

"Stevie," he begins hopefully, and rather directly, in consideration of what even he can see will be, by necessity, a short conversation, "I had to talk to you one more time. We won't be seeing each other anymore, and I didn't want things to end with my stupid behavior Saturday night." So much, but what next? He shuffles in the gravel. "To you this is silly, but to me you're important. I never . . . saw somebody that I liked so much. Right away, I mean." No, what does he mean? His thoughts, never very clear on this, are a mess right now. Helplessly he points to his own car. "I didn't even know I was gonna talk to you here, but when I saw you in person I was next to you in a second. Just like that. I didn't even know I would do it." He looks up expectantly, waiting for her to speak, like this last bit of information should be the last piece of the puzzle for her, like she has all the clues she needs with which she might formulate a response.

And she does. "It's not Stevie," she says. Then impatient with herself for being so condescending: "Of course you know that. My name's not really Stevie, it's Jennifer—Jenny."

He is stunned. It never occurred to him that her name wasn't Stevie. In fact he assumed that all the dancers really had those names. They seemed to fit so well—girls like that should be called by names like that—but maybe not. Maybe that's the point. "Jenny," he says. "I thought it was really Stevie. I'm such a dummy, I can't believe it. Do all the other girls have real names too?"

She finds this disarming and smiles as much as she dares: on his side. "Yeah. (laugh) At least as far as I know. What's the matter? Don't you like Jennifer?" What really could have happened last night? It's just as she thought: he's just a nice guy. Nothing more or less, a plain nice guy. Probably walked into the ladies' room purely by mistake and got tossed out so fast that he didn't have time to explain.

Not that they'd believe him, she thinks. Not that they'd even notice him in there, in the club, except just in time to throw him out. And this after giving her the rundown on whom to *let slide*. Hypocritical fucks. First night, Manager told her about the clipboard: ". . . now these guys, sometimes they get a little fucked-up and get outta line. We look the other way. You handle it however you want, but remember money is money, and if you're bugged by them touching you, you can always go and wash in the bathroom." This and the whole time she's thinking how she'll want to shower after just *talking* to that guy. Oh, fat Manager. Worse is that she knows not only would her boyfriend qualify for the clipboard, he'd insist on it.

"It's better, I think. I mean I like Stevie fine, but Jennifer is better. . . . It's beautiful." He feels the blush. Oddly, it comes as a welcome addition. "It's more like you. I like you."

"I like you too, Carroll," she laughs, and maybe she does. Enough, anyway, to say, "Hey, I gotta go to work, but if you want to meet me for coffee at Magpie's down there on the corner (she gestures with her arm) after work, well we could talk some more. I stopped there last week once on my way home; it's nice and tacky. I would probably be there tonight about . . . well, say between two-fifteen and two-thirty." What the hell, she can always bail if it turns out he mauled one of the girls last night.

First he can't believe it, then it seems too easy. After all this, it still seems too easy. He wonders if this ever happens to the other guys, or do they get better? Maybe coffee after work is the booby prize. Maybe all the girls all the time are going out with all the customers. They go out and laugh about him, about how he never went out with any of the girls. Stevie—Jennifer—is probably still too new to know that having coffee with Carroll is strictly taboo. Of course he knows better, but why would she want to have coffee with him? Truth be told, he never expected anything like this to ever happen. Watch Melissa some night, now there's a girl who'll set you straight about things. Thinks Melissa would rather take a bullet for the president than spend time with any of the jerks in this place, much less him. Coffee after work. Why would Stev—Jennifer—want to do that? What should he do?

"After work?" he says, hesitantly.

She laughs, too cute. "What's the matter?" she wants to know, but it's friendly, kidding-like. Whatever he wants, it's all a joke. This guy really is okay, and she's really got to get to work. "Don't you want me?"

Her words float over the gravel like feathers after a pillow fight. *Don't you want me?*

Does he?

* * *

Dark, but not really, he thinks, watching her walk into the club through the back door. In fact when you're back here and that door swings open, well if one of those spots is on the dancer then you really can see almost everything, for a second anyway. Could've saved a lot of money and just watched from out here every night. But then what would be the point in that?

Sour song grinds from crepitant gravel. Dust teased airborne by a parking car gets into his eyes, and when he rubs them they tear up. God's window wash, like those black guys who ask for quarters at stoplights after rubbing water and wadded newspaper around on your windshield: it's not about seeing better.

Carroll turns back toward his car. Two men walking to the club entrance pass him. They nudge each other, stop and turn around.

"Seen enough?" stupidly, one of them asks, over the giggles of the other.

Seen enough? thinks Carroll, slipping on the phrase, standing there in the dust with these men.

The words sound strange to him, like speaking in tongues, delirious, in the grip of some miscreant or pagan. Think about what you are, what there is to see. Not so hard anymore, you could walk away, like an intrepid buck, only smarter, on the highway, caught in a headlight. Seen enough?

"Seen enough?" says Carroll. "Is that the best you can do, I mean questionwise?"

The men laugh him off, suck into door. In—side.